A WHALE IN PARIS

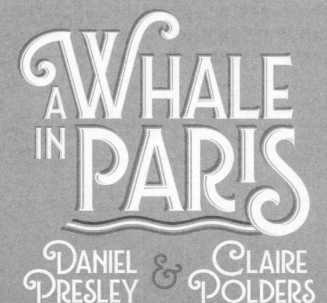

A WHALE IN PARIS

DANIEL PRESLEY & CLAIRE POLDERS

ILLUSTRATED BY

ERIN McGUIRE

HOW IT HAPPENED THAT
CHANTAL DUPREY BEFRIENDED A WHALE
DURING THE SECOND WORLD WAR
AND HELPED LIBERATE FRANCE

atheneum Atheneum Books for Young Readers

NEW YORK LONDON TORONTO SYDNEY NEW DELHI

ATHENEUM BOOKS FOR YOUNG READERS
An imprint of Simon & Schuster Children's Publishing Division
1230 Avenue of the Americas, New York, New York 10020

ATHENEUM BOOKS FOR YOUNG READERS is a registered trademark of Simon & Schuster, Inc. Atheneum logo is a trademark of Simon & Schuster, Inc.

For information about special discounts for bulk purchases, please contact Simon & Schuster Special Sales at 1-866-506-1949 or business@simonandschuster.com.

The Simon & Schuster Speakers Bureau can bring authors to your live event. For more information or to book an event, contact the Simon & Schuster Speakers Bureau at 1-866-248-3049 or visit our website at www.simonspeakers.com.

Interior design by Brad Mead
The text for this book was set in Odile.
The illustrations for this book were digitally rendered.
Manufactured in the United States of America
0418 FFG
First Edition
10 9 8 7 6 5 4 3 2 1
Library of Congress Cataloging-in-Publication Data
Names: Presley, Daniel, author. | Polders, Claire, 1976- author. | McGuire, Erin, illustrator.
Title: A whale in Paris / Daniel Presley and Claire Polders ; illustrated by Erin McGuire.
Description: First edition. | New York : Atheneum, [2018] | Summary: During the German occupation of Paris, Chantal, twelve, spies a whale while fishing with her father in the Seine and is determined to return it to the ocean before the Nazis or starving Parisians can destroy it.
Identifiers: LCCN 2017035841 (print) | ISBN 9781534419155 (hardcover : alk. paper) | ISBN 9781534419179 (eBook)
Subjects: LCSH: France—History—German occupation, 1940-1945—Juvenile fiction. | CYAC: France—History—German occupation, 1940-1945—Fiction. | Whales—Fiction. | Human-animal relationships—Fiction. | Single-parent families—Fiction. | World War, 1939-1945—France—Paris—Fiction. | Paris (France)—History—1940-1944—Fiction.
Classification: LCC PZ7.1.P73 Wh 2018 (print) | DDC [Fic]—dc23
LC record available at https://lccn.loc.gov/2017035841

For my parents
—D. P.

For Bert Barenholz (1931–2012),
who survived the war as a Jewish boy
—C. P.

SOUNDS AND SALMON

1

AN OUTLANDISH THRUM

The year was 1944 and the Germans had been the guests of Paris for nearly four years.

Well, not guests exactly, but that was what Papa called them. Chantal Duprey knew better than to take him seriously. After all, fathers use humor to hide the truth. Or spare your feelings. Or avoid difficult questions. Or cheer you up.

At least, *her* father did.

The night was the third of June, two weeks after her twelfth birthday, and Chantal was sitting in the dark beside Papa on the river's embankment, a fishing rod in her hand. Ever since the Germans became the "guests" of Paris, she and Papa had gone out after sunset to fish for salmon in the Seine. Winter or spring. At least three nights a week.

Papa was a fishmonger.

Before the war, fresh fish had arrived by the bucketful on trains and trucks from Normandy. The Duprey market cart was always full. Now, under the German occupation, they had to catch fish themselves.

Chantal stared at her unflinching line, the stubborn bobber floating on the surface. *Go on, fish, bite! Bite, I tell you.* She willed her bobber to sink, or even just to quiver. It wasn't working. No matter how much muscle she poured into her will, there was no ripple, no movement, no luck.

The night was still and stretching. As usual, Chantal and Papa didn't talk. They sat quietly side by side, wrapped up in their own minds.

In her mind was Mama, patiently teaching Chantal a new chord on the ukulele. What Papa was thinking was anyone's guess, but she assumed that her mother made an appearance in his mind too.

The bells of Notre Dame chimed the hour—midnight.

"Time to fill the bucket," Papa said.

"But we haven't caught any fish yet."

"They need to know that the bucket is full, and then they will come."

Chantal made her skeptical face. Papa always did this, sending her to the river's edge. *A smart girl like you shouldn't fear the water,* he often told her.

Papa didn't understand about the water and how it called to her in a sweet voice. A voice in her mind. Chantal never feared falling in. She feared that once she was in the water, she wouldn't want to leave it ever again.

It was in the water that Mama waited.

Chantal picked up the steel bucket and climbed down the sloping embankment. With the moon hiding behind a cloud, the Seine was practically black, prickling only with occasional torchlight from other anglers farther down on the opposite side of the river.

The water was low for this time of year. It hadn't rained much in April and May. Chantal wondered whether that was the reason they weren't catching any fish.

Are there fewer salmon in the river when the water is low?

Are the fish less likely to bite?

Chantal tied her rope to the bucket and lowered it into the river, careful not to clang it against the stone and scare potential fish away. She also made sure not to let the bucket sink too deeply, for if it did, the current would catch it, and the bucket would be heavy and difficult for her to haul up.

The moon emerged. She could make out the shapes of the roofs on the other side of the river. The windows of the houses were all dark because of the night patrols. Before the war, Paris had been known as the City of Lights. Now, all the street lamps were off, and the windows were blocked by curtains that had once been rugs or blankets.

The bucket filled with water, and more water, until it was time to reel it in. Just as she pulled the rope, she heard a deep rumbling sound coming from the water. A low thrum smudging the silence.

Her chest chilled as if she'd swallowed a chunk of ice.

This wasn't Mama's voice, the sweet voice Chantal usually heard in her mind. This voice was completely different. All of her concentrated on listening.

"Grrrrrooool-th-th-th!" echoed off the stone walls built high along the Seine.

The sound vibrated every nerve in her body.

"Who's there?" she asked.

The sound came again, louder. "Grrrrrooool-th-th-th!" An outlandish thrum so intense, it created a hole inside of her.

Frightened, she let the rope slip. The bucket plunged deep into the water and began traveling downstream.

"Oh no!"

Chantal held on to the rope and gave it a tentative tug. Nothing. She yanked and strained. The bucket wouldn't budge. Finally, she fastened her end of the rope to a metal cleat used to moor boats.

The rope went taut and shivered with tension.

Intrigued, Chantal plucked the rope. It gave off a low note, like the bass string of Mama's ukulele.

"Grrrrrooool," went the low sound in the water, as though in reply.

Impossible, she thought, squinting through the dark.

She plucked the rope twice.

"Grrrrrooool, grrrrrooool," went the sound, broadening and deepening between the stone embankments.

Where were the noises coming from? Chantal plucked the rope three times.

"Grrrrrooool, grrrrrooool, grrrrrooool."

She smiled. The sound that came from the darkness had a deep, friendly tone. Not the voice of a monster. There seemed to be good will in it. What could it be?

Four plucks.

"Grrrrrooool, grrrrrooool, grrrrrooool, grrrrrooool."

Chantal's smile changed to laughter. Whatever was out there obviously had a sense of humor. It laughed along with her until it faded and slurped away when another sound came. A much more upsetting sound.

Schomp! Bluck! Schomp! Bluck!

The clunk of heavy boots on cobblestones. Chantal looked up in alarm. Two dark shapes approached— German soldiers making their rounds. She felt her throat tighten in fear.

"Papa!"

She scrambled up the embankment and found him dozing, his face drawn tight around his bones. How defenseless he looked in the dark with his thin lips and stubbly chin. How different from the daytime Papa she knew, the broad-backed man who cooked and cracked jokes.

She shook him awake.

"What?" He sat up.

Chantal pointed in the direction of the soldiers. The Nazis' helmets were black and too dull to reflect the moonlight. Tall rifles swung with each clunking step. Dread on four legs.

Schomp! Bluck! Schomp! Bluck!

Papa climbed to his feet and waited beside Chantal. Seconds dripped past. They had all the permits they needed to be out after curfew. They were allowed to fish at night to provide for the city. And yet . . .

She seized his hand.

If the soldiers recognized them, all would be fine. But if the uniformed men were new recruits or felt like making trouble, Chantal and Papa would have to show their papers and answer all sorts of rude questions.

What are you doing here?

Who signed this permit for you?

Why is your daughter not in bed?

Where is her mother?

This last question was the trickiest. Chantal could answer it, but she preferred not to. She hoped the Germans would ask anything else, because whoever couldn't answer the questions quick enough risked being arrested or worse.

She had heard the stories. So many people imprisoned. Sent away. Shot.

Chantal closed her eyes and wished for the soldiers to be gone. Despite how much she hated them or lived in defiance of their presence, this was the way of the world now. Occupation. War.

There was no avoiding these "guests."

She opened her eyes again, and her stomach clenched. The two soldiers were now only a stone's throw away. The shorter one nodded like a gentleman and said, *"Bonsoir, monsieur. Bonsoir, mademoiselle."* (Good evening, sir. Good evening, miss.)

"Guten Abend, Herr Leutnant, Herr Feldwebel," Papa replied. (Good evening, Lieutenant, Sergeant.)

It was a game they played. The Germans pretended

they belonged in Paris and spoke French to show their good intentions. The Parisians, however, pretended to accept their fate and spoke German to show their contempt.

Chantal released a deep breath after the soldiers passed. But she didn't let go of Papa's hand until the echo of their boots had died away.

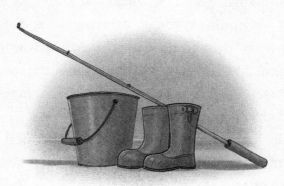

2

A Very Small Submarine

Chantal and Papa failed to catch a single fish that night. It was the first time such a thing had ever happened.

He blamed it on the drought.

On the nearly full moon.

On the soldiers.

He said the salmon just weren't in the mood.

Chantal considered his words with suspicion. How much of it was humor?

While they packed up their stuff to go home, Chantal worried about what Papa was going to sell that day.

A fishmonger could do without a knife. He could do without an apron. Without a loving wife. Yet a fishmonger without fish was like a boat without water.

Chantal and Papa climbed up the stone steps leading to the street-level quay. Rods over their shoulders, tackle box and empty bucket in hand.

On the horizon a pink dawn peeked. They had stopped fishing much later than usual, and Chantal was as hungry as a bear after a winter sleep. Though not as well-rested. She'd hardly slept at all. Her stomach growled loudly. Which reminded her . . .

"Papa, did you hear anything strange before the soldiers arrived?"

He shook his head.

"Nothing from the river?" she asked.

"What would I hear from the river?"

They crossed the street and walked to their apartment building—a whitewashed stone house, six stories high. Right on the Quai d'Orléans.

"I heard something. Earlier, when I went to put water in the bucket," she said.

"What?"

"A sound like a big moan."

"Probably a boat horn."

Chantal was unsure about this. Living on Île Saint-Louis, the smaller of the two islands in the Seine, she'd heard all the boat horns at least once, and none of them sounded like the moan she'd heard that night.

"You were sleeping," she said.

"Yes."

"So you didn't hear it."

"No."

Chantal bit her lip. "Maybe I thought . . ."

They went into their building and put down their fishing gear in a corner at the back of the communal hallway where other tenants parked their bicycles. Then they began their long climb up the stairs. Their apartment was on the top floor. No elevator.

"You thought what?" Papa asked.

First floor. Second floor. Up and up. Despite her fatigue, Chantal's imagination soared.

"The sound," she said. "Perhaps it was . . . *them.*"

By "them" she meant the British, the Americans— the Allies. Since the spring, the words "They're coming" popped up everywhere. Instead of *"Bonjour"* or *"Bonsoir,"* people would say *"Ils arrivent."* It was a secret code rolling off many tongues, a spark of hope on otherwise gloomy days: They're coming to free us.

"Them?" Papa said. "What about them?"

Third floor. *What if?* Chantal thought. *Could it be?*

"A submarine," she said. "Would they come in a submarine?"

Papa chuckled. "A submarine?"

Fourth floor. Muscles straining.

"Don't laugh."

Fifth floor. Panting. Her father paused and rubbed his face, reflecting on the idea. "It would have to be a very small submarine."

Sixth floor. Home.

THE WHITE NIGHTMARE

The apartment in which Chantal had lived for the whole of her life was composed of a living room, a small bedroom, and a makeshift kitchen. In the living room was a round table, a desk, a cupboard, a coal bin, two suitcases, a throw rug, and a collection of mismatched chairs.

Chantal's bedroom wasn't exactly a room. A sheet hung from a rope separating her space from the living room, where Papa slept on a daybed. Chantal's space was an alcove just wide enough for a bed and an armoire.

In the bottom drawer lived their most secret possession: the radio.

All in all, not much, but Chantal had a splendid view. If she climbed on her bed and stuck her head out the window, as she was doing right now, she could see buildings across the river that looked like giant cakes. If she faced right, she could see the gothic back of Notre Dame, the majestic cathedral with its spidery arches. If she looked down, there was the white-stoned bridge, Pont de la Tournelle. From there she could lose herself in the endless, dark flow of the Seine.

That night, or rather early morning, Chantal lay awake in her small bed by the window. In the wall behind her head she could hear the scampering of tiny feet. Mice.

Scippity-scrap. Scippity-scrap.

She didn't mind. If she concentrated on the skittish steps, if she listened closely enough, they might keep her awake. Like every night, Chantal was afraid of falling asleep, afraid of having the white nightmare.

In the white nightmare, she stood alone on a stone jetty, surrounded by a cottony field of mist as far as the eye could see. It was eerily quiet, as though she were the only soul alive. Out of the blanket of mist, white tendrils rose up, swirling, forming tongues that licked at her ankles and hands. She was seized by loneliness and an awful, traitorous desire to jump into that mist. Somehow she knew that in that blinding whiteness, she would sleep without fear and forget the pain of loss.

Each time Chantal awoke from the white nightmare, her pajamas would be drenched as though she'd been the one who'd drowned and not Mama. She hated this dream and had told no one about it. Not her father or Aunt Sophie. Not even her best friend, Odette.

Scippity-scrap. Scippity-scrap.

4

FRESH FISH

Chantal slept, dreaming not of white blankets of mist but of submarines so small you could fit them in your pockets like toys.

When she woke, Papa pressed a warm bowl into her hands—water steeped with chicory roots. Coffee and tea were in short supply.

"Drink up, *cherie!*" he said.

Chantal liked it when her father called her "*cherie.*" Who wouldn't want to be called "darling"? Each time

Papa said it, something warm was released into her blood, as warm as the chicory drink in her hands.

She joined him for breakfast in the kitchen, which wasn't far away. Only a long and a short step through the living room. In the kitchen was a stove, a rough wooden table, three chairs, and something quite special: an electric cool box.

There was also a calendar nailed to the wall. The day was Sunday, June fourth.

"I dreamed of submarines," Chantal told Papa as she sat at the table.

"Not that again," he said. "Eat your breakfast."

Breakfast consisted of stale bread and a peach that Papa presented like a fine meal. He cut the peach into slices and in between, he placed tiny sprigs of mint. To flavor the bread, he rubbed it with dried prunes. They'd already finished the butter for that week, and even the jar of strawberry jam Chantal had received from Father Maurice for her birthday was empty. She didn't complain as she sat on her chair, crunching her bread. She was used to getting by without the things she once thought essential.

Like hot croissants.

Hazelnut macarons.

The sound of Mama's voice.

Nobody had to tell Chantal that even though you

loved something (or someone) with all your might, it (or she) could always be taken away from you.

"Fresh fish!" Mama used to call. "Straight from the sea!"

Chantal remembered hearing these words again and again on countless mornings of her life.

"Fresh fish!"

It was the most wonderful thing. Walking up and down the narrow streets of Paris. The rattle of cart wheels on cobblestones. Ice tingling her fingertips. The clack of the scales. Money changing hands. The chatty customers lining up, their faces filled with happy anticipation.

Wherever Papa, Mama, and Chantal went with their cart of fresh fish, people from all over Île Saint-Louis would come in a hurry. The Duprey family had the freshest fish in all of Paris.

And why shouldn't they? Mama's sister, Aunt Sophie, brought it by the bucketful three times a week from Normandy.

Papa handled the fish: gutting it, boning it, filleting it. Chantal wrapped the purchases up in thick brown paper. Mama played her ukulele and sang.

Customers laughed and danced while waiting for their fish. How wonderful.

But when Chantal was seven years old, Mama disappeared in an accident at sea.

The world as Chantal knew it ended that day, and the world that replaced it was unrecognizable. The sun kept shining, but it didn't chase away the darkness.

There were no more songs as Papa pushed their cart through the streets. Instead, grief and longing followed them on their rounds, as though the emptiness Mama had left behind hung over their heads like a balloon on a string.

"Where did she go?" Chantal had sometimes asked.

Papa would hold her question in his eyes before placing his hand on her chest. "To your heart, *cherie*. That's where she went."

Chantal wasn't sure. If that was where Mama went, then why did the water call to her in such a sweet voice?

To bring life back to normal after Mama's death, Papa acted as though everything *was* normal, and Chantal played along. It was easier for both of them.

They learned how to be alone together, without a mother or wife to fill the space between them.

And life went on.

Chantal choked back her tears and acted happy. Day after day, she hid her sorrow until it became a natural reflex, like breathing.

But her true feelings were never gone for good. At night, they would surface in the form of the white nightmare.

FATHER MAURICE, MOTHER NATURE

After breakfast, Chantal put on her oldest and filthiest clothes—a brown corduroy dress, a man's shirt, green rubber boots.

She kissed her father on the nose and promised to be careful. "Yes, Papa, extra careful."

Down the six flights of stairs she went. Down was easy. Down was quick.

Although summer was on its way, the sky was white and the wind blustery, as if fall were coming instead.

Chantal crossed the street to look at the Seine, to

where she'd heard the musical moans last night. Had it been the call of a secret submarine? Or had her ears been playing tricks on her?

For a moment she imagined herself inside the submarine, onboard with the crew, gliding through the water unseen like a giant fish.

She cleared her throat and called down, hoping she'd hear the same sound again, the creaturely sound that was friendly.

"Hello?"

Nothing, of course. It was terribly unlikely that a submarine would keep the same hours and rounds as she did. Terribly unlikely, yet not inconceivable.

"Hello?"

Not one peep echoed from the Seine. Chantal continued on her way to Notre Dame.

Out of all the churches in Paris, Notre Dame was the most majestic and famous. It was the cathedral where Victor Hugo's hunchback rang the bells and Joan of Arc was made into a saint. It was also the parish of Father Maurice.

Chantal waited for him to notice her. He stood in his cassock below the arches that framed the massive oak doors, shaking hands with the worshippers. Sunday mass had just ended. The towers of Notre Dame aimed themselves at the sky.

"*Bonjour*, Chantal. So good to see you."

"*Bonjour*, Father."

Father Maurice was a man of spiritual sunshine. Even if you hadn't attended mass because you were too tired from fishing, his eyes were full of warmth and chocolate—the type of chocolate that melts easily in your hand.

"How is your father?" he asked.

"Very good, Father."

They giggled at her unintended joke.

Father Maurice motioned for her to follow him. They walked around the left side of the cathedral, the side that faced the Seine.

"And how is your aunt?"

Chantal turned to look at Father Maurice. Why was he always asking about Aunt Sophie? Because he couldn't ask about Mama, perhaps.

"I haven't seen her in a while, but I think she's doing fine."

Father Maurice opened the low gate that gave access to the public park behind the cathedral's spidery arches. He let Chantal slip inside ahead of him.

"Are you ready to get your hands dirty?" he asked.

Chantal nodded and put on her best smile. "How are the zucchinis doing?"

"I'm afraid they're not quite ready. But the fennel is coming in nicely."

Chantal hid her disappointment behind another smile, this one fake. She was waiting for the zucchinis. With them, Papa would make his super-delicious salmon quiche, which happened to be her favorite dish.

She walked beside Father Maurice on the gravel path toward the patches of cultivated earth behind Notre Dame. Fresh vegetables and fruits used to arrive on trains and trucks from all over France, but since the Germans stole most of the crops to feed their soldiers, Parisians had to grow their own food wherever they could.

It had been Father Maurice's idea to convert the park into a vegetable farm. The garden became his piece of paradise, a Garden of Eden, though not quite. New problems arose every day: too much sun, too much water, too many aphids, not enough time. The Miracle of Mother Nature was hard work.

They made their way down the rows of Swiss chard and Jerusalem artichokes, the mounds of earth with green sprigs aiming at the sky. *Much like the towers of Notre Dame,* Chantal thought.

Father Maurice unlocked the tool shed and gave Chantal a hand shovel, a pair of gloves, a watering can, a pair of pruning shears, and a sack. She glanced at the river.

"Father, I heard a strange noise coming from the Seine."

"Really? What did it sound like?"

Chantal did her best to imitate the outlandish thrum that had created a hole inside of her. "Grrrrrooool-th-th-th!"

Father Maurice leaned back, his eyes wide open. "Grrrrrooool-th-th-th?"

"Yes! So you heard it too?" If he had, surely Papa would believe her.

Father Maurice moved along without answering. Chantal hurried after him until they reached a group of volunteers already at work in the garden. Each of them greeted her warmly. She knew most of them by face but only half by name.

Should she ask Father Maurice again about the sound? No, he seemed too preoccupied.

Chantal got on her knees and dug into the soil. She breathed in the smell of ripe, churned earth, and focused on her tasks, which changed from day to day. When the sun beat down, she would water the vegetables and spread muslin overhead, a thin cloth to provide shade. When it rained, she would dig trenches to encourage the water to escape into the Seine.

Today, the weeds were crowding the turnips and an army of slugs was munching on the lettuce. She started with the slugs, peeling their slimy bodies off, one after another, and tossing them into a bucket. The leaves were left with holes, but Chantal knew the lettuce would survive.

Father Maurice's shadow fell over her. "Tell me," he said. "What would make a sound like that?"

So he *had* listened to her. Should she tell him more? In truth, she had no idea what had made the sound. She only knew what she wanted it to be.

"A submarine," she said.

"A submarine?"

Oh she had his attention now. "Yes. Think about it, Father. It could be *them*. What if they're coming?"

"In the Seine?" Father Maurice scoffed.

His loud words snatched her breath away. Everyone in the garden seemed to be staring at her.

"A submarine?" said a woman, sneering.

"In the Seine?" said someone else.

They all laughed.

Chantal swallowed hard, not meeting anyone's eye. A cry climbed in her throat.

6

CONQUERORS

For the rest of the day, Chantal said nothing more about the submarine. Not to Father Maurice or anyone. She concentrated on her weeding and harvesting. By late afternoon, her satchel was stuffed with a Savoy cabbage, half a kilo of green peas, three carrots, and one kohlrabi the size of her father's fist.

She headed home, a sense of achievement spiriting her step. Papa would be thrilled with all these vegetables. He would make something special for dinner every night of the week.

And that wasn't all. Chantal also proudly carried a trio of zucchinis in the crook of her arm, as you would a newborn baby.

Father Maurice hadn't been entirely honest with her. He had actually harvested the zucchinis the day before and, knowing how much Chantal loved them, had kept three back. Especially for her.

On Pont Saint-Louis, the bridge connecting the two islands, there was a painter at work. Chantal stopped to watch him, an old man with a red lump on his cheek the size of a snail. He looked out over the Seine. The brush in his hand was paused in the air. On his easel stood a painting with just a few blue lines. Waves, perhaps.

The picture was obviously unfinished, but there was something mysterious about it already. Something sad and solitary.

Was that how the painter felt? Or how he saw the world?

Chantal wondered and watched. The painter seemed on the verge of revealing a massive truth. She hoped to be there once the picture came to life. But today nothing was happening. The old man seemed lost in muted memories and blues.

Disappointed, she shrugged and was on her way.

Chantal loved art. Paintings, sculptures, and drawings had a magnetic effect on her. She missed visiting the Louvre. Of course the museum was still there, but its royal corridors were practically empty, its walls barren. Before the Germans had arrived, dozens of trucks had sped away from the museum with the most important works of art. No one knew where the Mona Lisa was hiding.

Chantal made a fist. How she hated the war. It had scared all the art away from the city.

She was eight years old when the German soldiers first marched down Avenue des Champs-Élysées. She remembered the sound, the mechanized thunder roaring in her ears.

Schomp! Bluck! Schomp! Bluck!

She was there on the sidewalk with Papa to watch them arrive. Along with the rest of Paris. Or rather, the people who hadn't fled the city ahead of time.

Chantal couldn't see a thing, short as she was. The sidewalk was a throng of bodies. No gap through which she could peek. For her, there was only the roaring sound.

Schomp! Bluck! Schomp! Bluck!

Chantal got curious about the men who won her city from the French. Were they as tall as giants? Did they have fangs for teeth? Coals for eyes?

She pulled her father's sleeve and asked if she could sit atop his shoulders, and Papa said yes. He made a step with his two hands, and Chantal clambered up and swung a leg around either side of his neck.

She couldn't believe her eyes. The line of muddy soldiers stretched all the way from the Arc de Triomphe to the obelisk on Place de la Concorde. A neverending stretch of brown uniforms and red flags.

"Papa! It's the entire German army!"

"No, *cherie*, just a part."

Impossible, thought Chantal.

She stared at the army filing past. Its movement was so regular and quick, the soldiers resembled a huge machine. She blurred her vision, then focused again until she saw faces, dirty and tired inside the helmets.

The soldiers didn't have any fangs that she could see. Nor were their eyes coals.

She only saw the faces of normal men, so young they were more like boys.

And they didn't seem angry. They looked around in awe.

"Papa! They came to see Paris!"

"No, *cherie*. They're not on holiday. They're our conquerors."

After the parade, she and Papa walked away from the Champs-Élysées, away from the crowd that had gathered to see these conquerors.

"Conquerors." The word made Chantal think of sword

fights and blood flowing down from mountains. She knew it even then: Human history is full of death and broken bones.

When she mentioned her thoughts to Papa, he began referring to their conquerors as their "guests."

7

A Table by the Window

ook at what I have," Chantal called out to Papa.

She unloaded her victory of vegetables on the kitchen table.

As predicted, Papa was thrilled. He picked up a zucchini and rolled it back and forth in his hands, testing its firmness. It was a gesture Chantal had seen him make a thousand times. "Better get cleaned up for dinner, *cherie*."

Chantal threw a towel over her arm, grabbed her bar of soap, and skipped out of the apartment. The bathroom was in the hall, shared with the others who lived on the floor.

At this hour, there was no line, but when she tried the bathroom door, it was locked. She sighed and crossed her arms.

Waiting for one neighbor was nothing. Waiting for several neighbors when she simply needed to wash wasn't a big deal either. What really annoyed Chantal was waiting in a meandering line when she desperately needed to pee.

There was an old-fashioned chamber pot Papa kept under his daybed, in case of a real emergency. Still, there were privacy issues to consider. Plus something called hygiene. Chantal avoided using the chamber pot as much as she could.

When the bathroom door finally unlocked, she moved to the side to make space.

"*Bonsoir, Chantal. Ça va?*" (Good evening, Chantal. How are you?)

She smiled politely. The man who stepped out in his bathrobe was Professor Petit, her sixth-grade teacher, who lived in the last apartment on the right.

"*Ça va bien, Maître Petit. Et vous?*" (I'm fine, Mr. Petit. And you?)

His face was small and not unlike a mouse's. But the most remarkable thing was that Professor Petit had been born with only one complete arm. His other arm ended where the elbow should have been.

Chantal found it hard not to stare at her teacher's missing arm. Which always made her wonder: Can you stare at something that isn't there?

Scrubbed clean from top to toe, Chantal joined Papa in the kitchen.

The smells that circled from the stove up into her nostrils were warm, like love itself.

Chantal offered to help with dinner, and Papa asked her to shell the peas, which she did at the table. She liked pressing her fingernails into the seams of the pods and hearing the green beads pop into the ceramic bowl.

Above the table hung pictures of Mama and Papa. Mama and Chantal. Mama and Papa and Chantal. Mama and Aunt Sophie. Mama and Chantal and Aunt Sophie—the scenes of one photograph spilling into another.

None of the pictures showed all four of them together.

This photograph did exist, though. Chantal had seen it. She knew Papa had taken the picture down after Mama died. She even knew why. Her father and Aunt Sophie didn't see eye to eye. They fought at times, and otherwise kept their distance. What Chantal didn't know was how to bring them back together.

"Would mademoiselle care for a table by the window

or near the *cuisine* (kitchen)?" Papa asked, sprinkling salt into the pot.

"The window, monsieur, with a view of the Seine."

That night, like every night, Chantal and Papa performed their dinner theater. He pretended to welcome her into a luxurious restaurant, and she pretended to be a customer seduced by the menu featuring salmon in all its varieties. Whenever they caught more salmon than they could sell, Papa put the extra fish in the cool box and, when the time came, cooked them up for dinner.

Unfortunately, the super-delicious salmon quiche was not on the menu tonight, because they had no more ration tickets for eggs.

Chantal remembered the first time she and Papa had stood in line at Lambert's *boulangerie* (bakery) like everyone else, studying their ration tickets. Only one loaf of bread a week for both of them?

"That's not enough to live on!" Papa had said.

It was Father Maurice who'd replied: "Then we must make do."

For Parisians "making do" amounted to different things. Papa and Chantal fished in the Seine. Father Maurice grew vegetables behind his cathedral. Odette, Chantal's best friend, received potatoes in the mail from her uncle who farmed in the country. But there were other, more dangerous methods for getting food. Aunt

Sophie frequented the black market. Some people caught pigeons in the Jardin des Tuileries. Professor Petit was raising a herd of guinea pigs at home. There was also talk of cats and dogs being kidnapped.

At the Duprey table with a view of the Seine, dinner didn't include any dogs, cats, or guinea pigs. Thankfully. Before Chantal was a new dish Papa had invented: *Saumon de l'Alsace* (salmon with steamed cabbage, peas, and carrots). Papa had saved the zucchinis for when eggs would be available again.

She ate as slowly as possible, savoring each bite. The cool box was almost empty.

8

SALMON SERENADE

After dinner, Chantal did the dishes while Papa prepared for curfew by closing the shutters.

Outside, the sky grew dark.

They put on their pullovers and grabbed their blankets, getting ready to go out. Chantal hoped they would catch the fish they desperately needed.

Down the six flights of stairs they went.

Along with the tackle box, Chantal brought her ukulele to the bank of the Seine.

The instrument was beautiful. Its pegs were made of

ivory and carved into the flukes of a tail fin. A mother-of-pearl inlay spread across the fret board like a spray of fine seaweed.

It was the fisherwoman's ukulele that once belonged to Mama.

"A salmon serenade?" Papa said, noticing the ukulele in Chantal's hand. He was carrying the steel bucket and the cane fishing rods.

Chantal made no response. She wasn't planning on serenading the salmon, but perhaps it was best for her father to think so.

They stopped at the spot where they always fished and put their gear down on the stones.

Chantal opened the tackle box and removed a hook with its green feathery lure. She unwrapped the fish eggs from the waxed paper.

Papa loaded both of their hooks and cast the lines into the water. He secured the end of the rods into iron rings attached to the stone walls of the embankment.

They fished for a while, yet nothing happened. The hours hobbled on.

Chantal waited for Papa to fall asleep. As soon as he did, she set down her fishing rod and moved closer to the water, bringing the ukulele with her. She tried to recall the exact note the rope had made the previous night.

Was it a D?

She strummed a D major chord, then cocked her head to listen.

Nothing.

Perhaps a C?

She strummed the chord and . . .

"Grrrrrooool-th-th-th!" echoed off the stone walls.

"The submarine!"

Should she wake Papa? Part of her wanted him to hear what sounded like bellows breathing in the dark. Another part of her wanted to keep the submarine to herself. There was something so special about what was happening that she wasn't quite ready to share it.

She regarded her hand on the ukulele's neck, her fingers still shaped in a C major. It occurred to her that C major was the first chord of a new song she had been practicing—an American song called "Somewhere Over the Rainbow." It came from a film about a wizard who lived in an emerald city. Chantal had never seen the film, but she remembered the posters hanging in Paris from when she was little.

What was the second chord?

First it was C major and then came an E minor. Chantal played the second chord.

"Grrrrrooool," went the sound from the river, its pitch slightly changed, harmonizing with the ukulele.

Was a submarine singing to her ukulele? If so, where was it?

Chantal squinted into the darkness.

There, on the opposite side of the river, close to the bank, she spotted something: great currents of water sloshing one over the other.

Chantal narrowed her eyes even more. She struggled against the inkiness until she saw it again: a dark shape that looked like the polished back of a seal. A very big seal. The shape slid and twisted into long curves and streaks of reflected light. Soon it was gone again, disappearing into the water.

Something sparked inside Chantal's head. Her heart fluttered with excitement as the blood rushed through her veins.

What she had seen was not a very small submarine.

Nor was it a very big seal.

What she had seen was a whale. A whale in the Seine.

"Papa, come and look!"

She could no longer keep something so massive to herself and had rushed back to where her father lay sleeping, higher up the embankment.

"What?" Papa opened his eyes in dreamy confusion, yet gathered himself quickly.

Chantal took his hand and pulled him up. "Come and look."

At the river's edge, she explained what she'd seen.

"Impossible," was his response.

"No, Papa. You have to believe me. There is a whale out there."

"First a submarine, and now a whale."

In the dark, they watched the water's surface for a good long time. There was nothing but smooth black lines, rippling.

He wrapped an arm around her shoulder. "A whale is not a salmon," he said. "It would never swim up the Seine."

"Maybe it was chasing salmon and took a wrong turn?"

Papa petted her head as though she were a much younger child. "Yes, *cherie*. Like France. Like all of us."

Chantal disliked it when her father petted her head like that. It meant she was being too silly to be taken seriously.

She shrugged off his arm and returned to their fishing gear and blankets.

Mama would have believed her. She was sure of it.

That night, for the second time in a row, they caught no salmon. Not one miserable fish. Walking home, Chantal couldn't stop thinking about the almost-empty cool box in the kitchen. Neither she nor Papa had any fat left on their bones. Could they survive on rations and Father Maurice's vegetables alone?

Later, in bed, Chantal buried her face into her pillow so Papa wouldn't hear her cry. Nights were always the hardest. Shadows pulling at her from all sides. Loneliness thriving.

In the dark, it was impossible to miss Mama only a little.

PRIVATE SCHRÖDER

The next day was Monday, June fifth. Like every Monday, Chantal walked to school, yawning, her books in a burlap rucksack on her back. She waited under the chestnut tree on a square that was technically a triangle. It was their spot, hers and Odette Lambert's.

Should she tell Odette about the whale? Would her best friend believe her?

Odette arrived with her shocking mop of red hair and eyes that looked like pools: big, blue, and watery.

They kissed each other's cheeks, or rather the air

around them. They chatted about the weekend, but Chantal didn't mention the whale. First she would need more proof.

"Oh, I almost forgot," Odette said, digging through her book bag. Out came a small wax paper sack from her parents' *boulangerie*.

"Odette, you are the sweetest."

Chantal peeled open the waxy sack. Inside was a croissant, flattened. Its buttery scent made her mouth water.

Odette winked. Whenever she had smushed or crushed or mangled one of her parents' pastries, she brought it to Chantal, who always shared it with Papa.

A klutz for a best friend has its advantages.

School was a terrible bore.

"One more week until summer holiday," Odette whispered, sitting beside Chantal in the classroom.

Chantal shrugged. What was a summer holiday in times of war?

She struggled to stay awake. Two back-to-back nights of luckless fishing had exhausted her. Fortunately, it didn't matter because in the early morning, Professor Petit taught German, that ugly language of the conquerors she had no desire to learn.

Halfway through the lesson, there was a knock on the door.

"*Ja?*" Professor Petit said. "I mean, *oui*—yes?"

The door opened. On the threshold stood Private Schröder, his rifle slung over a shoulder. The school and its grounds fell under the vigil of this one German soldier, a young private with no stripes. A private whose teeth were too big for his mouth. In an effort to mask this flaw, he had tried to grow a mustache, which was so wispy it didn't do much masking at all.

Chantal knew him to be a severe soldier, his face tight with concentration and resolve. He took off his helmet and cleared his throat. "I would like to have a word with your class, monsieur."

The private's French was quite good, almost as good as her teacher's German.

Professor Petit gave a reluctant nod.

Private Schröder put a hand on his gun and turned to face the class. "I am here to execute an order."

Chantal and her classmates held their breath. German orders were never good news.

During the past four years, there had been many nasty surprises resulting from German orders. Teachers and children had disappeared overnight. One morning, Chantal arrived to find empty seats in her classroom. On another morning, two classes needed to be combined because a teacher had been taken away.

It was said that some people had fled the city, went into hiding, or were deported.

Especially the Jewish people.

Chantal had witnessed the terrible consequences of Hitler's bigotry and hatred. How the Jews had been forced to identify themselves with yellow stars on their clothing, even the girls and boys at her school. How the Jews had been barred from public places such as parks and swimming pools. How they'd been forbidden to travel. How their shops and doctors' offices had been obliged to close.

All brought on by German orders.

You could still see those empty buildings, padlocked, burned down, or painted with black swastikas—that ugly symbol the Nazis used to instigate fear.

Almost two years ago, in a violent raid, thirteen thousand Jews had been rounded up by the French police on German orders.

Most of them were women and children.

They were sent to concentration camps, to Auschwitz. From Aunt Sophie, Chantal knew the horrifying truth. No one returned from these camps. The Jewish people were sent there to work and die.

In the classroom, on this fine June morning, Private Schröder clicked his heels. What would the German orders be today?

He handed Professor Petit a letter along with his credentials. "We have received a report of possible enemy maneuvers. I am here to take an informer in for questioning."

"An informer," Professor Petit repeated in quiet defiance. He was not one for drama and kept his cool.

"Yes, monsieur."

"Look around this classroom and tell me, what do you see?"

Chantal and her classmates stared at the two men in front of the blackboard. Attention had never been so fierce.

"Excuse me?" the private said.

"It's a simple question. What do you see?"

There was something weary and indecisive in the private's face that didn't match his uniform, all neat and crisp and sharp.

"I . . . I . . . see children."

"Exactly. I do not have any 'informers' in my classroom," said Professor Petit. He was not intimidated. Perhaps he was drawing on a secret power.

Chantal imagined his missing arm to be as strong as a gorilla's, keeping the soldier at bay.

Professor Petit passed the private's letter back to him. "You have interrupted us long enough. Don't you want the children to learn German?"

"I am looking for Chantal Duprey," Private Schröder blurted.

What? In one blow, Chantal was paralyzed. Floored, with an elephant sitting on her chest. What should she do?

Private Schröder walked up and down the aisles, the butt of his rifle knocking against each desk as he passed.

"Where is she, this girl?"

Chantal looked down at the dirty classroom floor. How her heart was beating! Nearly out of her chest. Breathing became an Olympic sport.

"Everyone. Identity papers on your desk. Now!"

Slowly, very slowly, her classmates began to move. Even Odette bent down to search for her papers in her book bag.

Chantal glanced up at Professor Petit. His invisible arm was no longer powerful. This was a helpless man if ever there was one, a man who couldn't protect her.

"I'm here," she said, standing.

"Sit back down," Professor Petit said.

It was too late. She had identified herself. Private Schröder marched over and stopped in front of her.

"Chantal Duprey?"

"Yes, monsieur."

"The Chantal Duprey who has seen a submarine in the Seine?"

Murmurs raced around the classroom. Chantal trembled. So that's what they wanted. The Germans thought she had information on the British and the Americans. *Possible enemy maneuvers.*

How stupid of her to have said anything. Why couldn't she have kept the submarine to herself? But wait, it wasn't a submarine after all. It was . . .

"A whale."

"What?" barked Private Schröder.

"What's this about?" Professor Petit said, moving down the aisle toward them.

"Well," Chantal managed to say, "it wasn't *really* a submarine."

"That's not what I heard," Private Schröder said. "Come with me."

He extended his hand as though to grab her arm, but Professor Petit squeezed himself between Chantal and the private, his back toward her, facing the German.

Petit: "She's not going anywhere."

Schröder: "Step aside, monsieur."

Chantal: "It was a whale."

Petit: "Be quiet, Chantal."

Schröder: "A whale?"

Petit: "Don't listen to her."

Chantal: "There is no submarine in the Seine. It's a whale."

Private Schröder took a step back and Professor Petit turned around so that both men were facing her now. She wasn't sure, but she thought a few of her classmates laughed.

"Listen," Professor Petit said. "Chantal didn't mean any harm. She's a silly girl. Her mother died a few years ago, and ever since, well . . . her head's been full of make-believe. One day she said a rat had gotten into the classroom. I sent the children outside in the cold and searched the room but found nothing but a carton of broken Easter eggs."

Chantal recalled the rat that Professor Petit had indeed not found. She also recalled Odette dropping the carton of eggs on her way to school from her parents' *boulangerie*.

Odette had cried, "Oh no! Everyone will hate me."

"Don't worry," Chantal had told her. "I have an idea."

Chantal was quick with ideas, although now that she was facing a German soldier in class, she had none.

"You're saying the girl is a liar?" Schröder asked.

"No. I'm saying don't let a silly girl's fantasies get the best of the German army."

Private Schröder took that last sentence under consideration. He gave his head a rueful shake. Then, in three tall strides of his boots, he was out of the classroom and gone.

ARE WE IN TROUBLE?

Chantal had not cried during the whole episode, but the moment the classroom door closed behind the German private, tears pooled in her eyes and ran down her cheeks, tears from fright and rage and who knows what.

Odette got up, also in tears, and wrapped her arms around her friend. There they stood, a bundle of soft, entangled limbs. Their shoulders heaved in sync.

"Chantal." It was Professor Petit's voice.

"Yes?" she said, from somewhere inside Odette's arms.

"Maybe you want to go home?"

Chantal rushed through the streets, anxious to tell her father what had happened. She flew down the river quay and up the six flights of stairs.

She was panting when she finally arrived home. About to burst into the apartment, Chantal heard voices coming from inside. She held back. Were the German soldiers here too?

She placed her cheek against the door and imagined her ear becoming a giant ear. She strained it until she recognized the second voice. It belonged to Aunt Sophie. What a surprise!

Chantal opened the door wide.

"Aunt Sophie," she said, dashing in and throwing her arms up for an embrace.

Sophie's face lit up as she hugged Chantal. Chantal breathed in her aunt's scent: the spice of cork and clove, the sharp bite of iodine—no one in the world smelled the same.

No one in the world *was* the same.

Aunt Sophie was like a heroine in a movie: the look of her, her obvious preoccupation with secrets. The strong lines along the sides of her jaws. The way she shook hands. A handshake like a nutcracker, people said.

"Why are you home from school?" asked Papa, interrupting their embrace.

Chantal released Sophie and faced Papa. She began her tale. With each part of the story—how the German soldier had come into the classroom, how he had asked for her, how he had wanted to take her in for questioning, how Professor Petit wouldn't let him—she felt the room chill.

"I don't understand," Papa said. "Why did they want to question you?"

"The submarine."

"The submarine?" Aunt Sophie asked.

"She means the whale," Papa said to Sophie.

Sophie's eyes grew wide. "I'm lost. Could someone please tell me what's going on?" She reached up a hand to brush the hair out of Chantal's eyes.

Sophie's touch calmed her. Papa never touched her in such a way. Only Mama had. Chantal explained about the sounds she'd heard from the river. "At first I thought it was a submarine. But I was wrong. It's a whale."

"A whale?" said Aunt Sophie.

If only people could stop saying that! Chantal thought.

"How did the Germans find out?" Papa asked.

That was a good question. After a moment of thought, Chantal presented an equally good answer: "I told the people in the garden. The volunteers, before I knew the submarine was actually a whale."

"What did I say?" Papa growled at Chantal. "Don't

stand out. Don't draw attention. Don't give the Germans any excuse to single you out."

"You told whom exactly?" Sophie asked Chantal, seeming more than casually interested in the reply. If she were a dog, her ears would have pricked up right about now.

Chantal took a moment to think again, yet this time her answer was insufficient. "I don't know. There were a lot of people. I only know half of them by name. . . . It was silly of me to say anything." Silly was what Professor Petit had called her. "Are we in trouble?"

"That depends," Sophie replied. "Did you tell them about . . . ?"

Chantal knew what Sophie meant—the radio. The radio the size of a breadbox, covered in varnished walnut with four large knobs beneath an illuminated panel. The radio they were not allowed to have. The radio that was very, very illegal.

"No, I didn't mention it."

"Or something you might have heard on it?" Sophie asked. "A broadcast?"

Chantal's mind was spinning so fast, it almost made her dizzy.

"Think, Chantal, think!"

"Sophie," Papa warned. "This is not an interrogation."

"I'm sorry, but I need to know," Sophie insisted, softening. "It's important."

"No," said Chantal.

"No, what?"

"No, I said nothing about the radio or the broadcasts."

Sophie breathed a sigh of relief. She took Chantal's chin in her hand, not roughly but with a certain authority, and said, "Don't go around spreading any more fantastical stories. You'll only bring attention to yourself. No more stories, hear?"

Chantal would have nodded if her chin had not been clenched inside her aunt's hand.

"I'm sorry."

Sophie released her. "It's okay," she said. "It's not your fault."

Only the two of them knew the world that was present in such simple words.

Not your fault.

11

NOT YOUR FAULT

t's not her fault," Mama used to say.

"Then whose fault is it?" yelled Papa.

"Calm down, Henri. I'm sure there's an explanation."

"An explanation? You always take her side."

Mama and Papa would sometimes argue about Aunt Sophie. It was Sophie's job to catch the fish in Normandy and bring them to Paris, where it was Mama's and Papa's job to sell them. They split the money three ways.

"It's a crisis!" Papa would say whenever the fish didn't arrive on time.

Eventually, Mama could no longer defend Aunt Sophie. "I will go to Normandy and see what's wrong."

Chantal was only seven at the time and didn't want to be separated from her mother. She pleaded with her to be taken along.

So Mama did.

Together they traveled to Honfleur, the coastal town where Mama and her sister had grown up. They found Aunt Sophie in a gloomy state. Her bad mood had something to do with all the empty bottles strewn about her small house. In them used to be beer, whiskey, rum, cider, and apple brandy.

Chantal helped her mother collect all the empty bottles and take them away. They found bottles that weren't empty hidden in the basement. These they poured down the sink.

Aunt Sophie became furious. Chantal hardly recognized her. She was thin and frail looking, as though she'd stopped eating in favor of drinking. Her breath was bad, and she smelled as sour as the bar she was constantly in. She spent more time there than on the boat, a boat that needed a great deal of maintenance.

A boat named *Victoire*, a small diesel trawler.

Mama went into every place in town and told the bartenders, "If Sophie comes in here, serve her a glass of milk and nothing else."

They did what Mama said.

Chantal and Mama cooked big meals for Aunt Sophie and made certain she got plenty of rest. Slowly, her strength and wry sense of humor returned. When they weren't repairing her, Chantal and Mama repaired the boat and mended the nets.

After two weeks, the *Victoire* was shipshape, though Sophie was not. She was still shaky and in no condition to fish. Mama couldn't wait any longer. Their customers on Île Saint-Louis were depending on the Duprey family.

She put on her canary slicker and kissed Chantal on the forehead. "Somebody's got to catch the fish, *cherie*."

There should have been nothing to worry about. Mama used to fish all the time, before she married Papa, before she became Mama.

But Chantal was worried. "There's a storm coming."

"I'll be back before it strikes."

Mama's face was beautiful, her bright eyes shining with hope for every challenge she tackled. As long as Mama was there, anything was possible.

Chantal helped her carry the fishing rods and the mended nets to the stone jetty. The last thing she handed over was Mama's Breton cap, dark blue and made of wool.

She watched Mama ease away and float out into the harbor in the renovated *Victoire*. She stayed behind until Mama's lantern was only a speck on the horizon.

When Chantal returned to the house, Aunt Sophie wasn't there.

Chantal listened to the radio while waiting for her aunt to return. The weatherman said the storm was moving fast, faster than expected. Chantal was sure Mama had been aware of this. Her mother was a Norman *and* a fisherwoman. She could read the sky and the wind like an expert mariner.

Chantal didn't worry until the rain began to pelt Aunt Sophie's tin roof. It sounded as if giants were throwing pebbles down from the sky. Chantal realized it wasn't rain, but hail.

She hurried into her slicker and grabbed a small cooking pot to place on her head. By now, Mama would be on her way back in, and she would need help bringing the fish out of the boat.

Outside, the storm was fierce. The rain and hail pelted against Chantal's makeshift helmet. Under the slicker, she felt her shoulders and arms bruising beneath a thousand jabs.

In the port, she paced up and down the stone jetty, furious with impatience. If Chantal were the type of child who frequently cried, she would have then, but it wasn't in her character.

The storm began to ease. The hail stopped and the rain faded to a mist.

The mist drifted over the water and blanketed the town. The stone jetty upon which Chantal stood was soon surrounded by a cottony field as far as the eye could see. Street lamps that distantly ringed the harbor were no more than dimmed lights orbiting her. Planets glowing with an underwater shine.

White tendrils rose up out of the blanket of mist, swirling, forming tongues that licked at her ankles and hands.

Chantal became very afraid.

She thought about running back into town, but what if the town was gone? One step into all that boiling steam would be her undoing. Off the jetty she'd fall, into an abyss.

A dark shape cut through the mist and headed toward her, from the direction of the open sea. Her mother's boat?

Chantal rushed up to the very end of the jetty, careful not to slip over the edge and into the eternal cloud.

She crouched and waited, shaking. The dark shape became more and more defined as it drifted forward. She could make out the bow of a boat and perhaps the shadow of a mast and a boxy cabin. Was it the *Victoire*?

Chantal's heart began racing.

The boat drew closer.

The mast ended in jagged splinters.

The boat drew closer still.

It knocked against the jetty.

And knocked.

Empty.

Was it the right boat?

Chantal lay on her stomach and reached out her hand as far as she could. Her fingers brushed against a rope coiled on the keelson. She turned her body into an elastic band and stretched a bit farther, managing to grab hold of the rope.

Once she had the rope fastened to a cleat on the jetty, Chantal climbed aboard and combed through the craft.

The cabin was small, unable to hide anyone. She investigated the rest of the boat. The hail had severely damaged it. Pellet-sized gouges had been torn out of the bow. In some places, digs the size of walnuts had been hollowed out of the foot braces.

Her mother was nowhere to be seen.

Her fishing rods, yes, and the tackle, but no Mama. Chantal recognized the nets she'd mended. And, worst of all, her mother's Breton cap.

She turned it over in her hands. The blue wool was frayed and slightly tattered in places, as though the poor hat had been kicked down the street. It was the same hat, though. Chantal was certain.

It was the right boat.

Chantal rushed back to the house. Aunt Sophie would fix this. She would know where Mama had gone and bring her back. But Chantal found Sophie in the same state as weeks earlier—staggering, singing softly to the radio, her voice slurred.

She was in no condition to fix anything.

Together they returned to the stone jetty. Aunt Sophie, even in her drunken state, quickly identified the *Victoire*. There was no mistake. It was their boat.

Chantal and her aunt waited for day to break. When it did, Aunt Sophie asked every fisherman and fisherwoman whether Mama had been spotted or seen boarding another craft. Time and time again she asked. All she and Chantal ever received in reply were grave looks of concern accompanied by the same answer: No.

After two hours of this, Aunt Sophie started crying and muttering, "What have I done?" Chantal had never seen her aunt cry before, and to witness it was horrible. Horrible because it made her mother's disappearance real. Chantal had truly believed Mama would be back by now. Her aunt's sobbing, however, told a different story, a story Chantal was unprepared to hear.

Her mother, gone?

Chantal could scarcely believe it. The horror of never seeing Mama again. Her bright, confident eyes gone forever. The courage beaming from her face swallowed by the sea.

For months, Chantal hoped for her mother's return. It was impossible that Mama had ceased to exist. To Chantal, Mama was still there, floating in the atmosphere, among the elements, and most particularly, under the water.

After the accident, Aunt Sophie never touched another drop of alcohol. She made a promise to Chantal and kept that promise.

A promise is a solemn thing and should never be taken lightly.

A promise can make you forgive.

"It's not your fault," Chantal told her aunt over and over again.

Not your fault.

12

IT'S HAPPENING

After Chantal told Papa and Aunt Sophie about what had happened at school with Private Schröder, the three of them shared Odette's flattened croissant. It was scrumptious.

Sophie put on her jacket.

"Where are you going?" Chantal asked.

"Sorry, *ma chou*," said Sophie. "Top secret, but I'll be back for dinner."

Chantal went downstairs and outside with her aunt. She waved good-bye and went to the river, where she sat down on the edge of the quay, feet dangling. Below her, the water rushed along as usual. Green and murky. There was nothing moving in the river, no dark shape that looked like the polished back of a whale.

In her mind, Chantal went back over the last two nights. There had been a real exchange between her and the whale. She was sure of it. The creature had tried to communicate with her. The plucked rope. The strange sounds. Her ukulele and the whale's echo.

Chantal considered the possibility that meeting the whale wasn't a coincidence. If it were a coincidence, it would have happened only once. But she'd heard the whale twice, on two consecutive nights.

Perhaps the whale was some kind of sign to be taken seriously. Some kind of destiny. And when destiny calls, you have to answer. What if the whale had swum all the way to Paris to warn her about something?

Aunt Sophie returned that evening, carrying a bundled handkerchief. Her face radiated triumph. "Look at what I have!"

She opened her handkerchief, and Chantal peeked inside: eggs! A full dozen.

Papa came in from the hall. "Is everything all right?"

"Everything is more than all right," Sophie said. Her

smile grew until it became as large as a melon slice. "It's happening, Henri. It's really happening."

"Are you sure?" Papa asked, his face lit up with golden light.

"I just heard the confirmation. Yes, I'm sure."

"What's happening?" Chantal asked.

Papa and Aunt Sophie exchanged a look heavy with meaning. So much talking without talking!

"What's happening is," Papa said, his eyes darting to Sophie's bundle of eggs, "I'm making my super-delicious salmon quiche!"

Chantal knew that this was not what her father and aunt had been talking about, but she couldn't help feeling excited. After all, salmon quiche was her favorite dish. She always watched carefully how it was made.

HENRI DUPREY'S SUPER-DELICIOUS SALMON QUICHE RECIPE

& *First make the crust with flour and water, and rub in some butter with your fingertips. It helps to sing while you do this. Singing, or humming if you can't keep a tune, helps the dough stay pliant and moist.*

& *Pat the pastry into a round tart tin. Make certain there are no holes or tears. Tighten your face with* concentration. Be sure to snap your fingers twice after trimming the overhanging pastry with a letter opener or other object of sentimental value that doesn't belong in a kitchen. Add anise and sugar (if available) to the leftover pastry and later make into cookies.

  Light the oven. While doing this, say "Voilà!" like a vaudeville magician.

  Bake the crust, and in another pan, bake the salmon filet for fifteen minutes, but not before thanking the salmon for jumping onto the hook.

  In a saucepan, sauté the zucchinis with herbs de Provence and salt. Read the newspaper.

  While whistling, crack the eggs into a bowl and whip them with a fork. Make sure the yolks streak the white with yellow. More salt. Do not throw away the eggshells! They can be used as tiny pots for starting plants from seeds. Afterward, the shells can be scattered in the garden to scare away slugs and snails.

  Remove the crust and the salmon from the oven. Compliment the filet and fork it into soft, steamy flakes. Don't forget to taste a bite or two or three. Add the salmon and the cooked zucchinis to the eggs and pour the whole thing into the crust. Add even more salt, some pepper. Sneeze.

❧ Bake the quiche until it's firm. Serve with a flourish, as though you've created something magical. You have.

Chantal and Sophie sat around the kitchen table as Papa served the quiche. Chantal wouldn't let her aunt slice into it until the delectable steam had been consumed first. The nose must be fed before the belly.

While they ate, Chantal's mind traveled back to the whale. How could she convince Papa and Aunt Sophie of what she'd seen? "Do whales eat salmon?" she asked.

"Sure they do," Sophie said. "I bet they eat a lot."

Papa made a dismissive gesture. "*Cherie*, please."

"But if a whale eats salmon," Chantal said, "then that's the proof!"

Aunt Sophie leaned back and crossed her arms. "Proof of what?"

"That what I saw was real. Last night in the Seine. It was a whale."

"Be honest," Papa said. "You don't know what you saw. It was dark."

"You were sleeping," said Chantal in her blaming voice. She turned to Sophie. "The whale made a sound too. A growl like this: 'Grrrrrooool-th-th-th!'"

Chantal gave her best imitation of the sound she'd

heard on both nights, which made Sophie laugh. Which made Chantal laugh. Which made Papa laugh. It reminded Chantal how good laughing could make you feel.

When they were done laughing, Chantal became serious again. "Tell her, Papa, how much salmon we caught these last two nights."

Her father looked as though he was about to say something humorous. One of his typical jokes. In the end, however, he said nothing at all.

After dinner, Sophie went into the hallway to use the bathroom, and Chantal prepared to go out fishing.

"Not tonight, *cherie*," Papa said. "You need a good night's sleep."

"But the whale . . . What if it's waiting for me?"

"Then it will have to wait for you until tomorrow."

Chantal pouted. It was hard to argue with her father. His decisions were always final. She looked forward to the day when hers would be the voice of authority.

Papa motioned for her to come over. She did and he pulled her onto his lap. She was too old to be sitting on her father's lap, yet it wasn't easy to stop doing something that felt right. She could guess what was coming. Not the words exactly, but the weight of them. Whenever Papa wanted to tell her something big, he would pull her close and hug her. It made it easier for him.

"You know I love you more than anything in the world, right?" Papa whispered in her ear.

Chantal rubbed her head against his chest. "I love you too, Papa."

"I just want you to be healthy and safe. You are everything to me. Everything."

When Sophie returned, Chantal suggested she take her bed for the night.

"No way, ma chou," Sophie said with a wink. "But there's something else you could do for me."

"What?" Chantal asked, watching her aunt arrange some cushions on the floor to serve for her bed.

"Play us a song?"

Chantal didn't feel like playing a song, but given how kind Sophie had been for bringing the eggs, and the magnificence of the quiche, it was impossible to refuse.

She took up her ukulele and began picking the chords of "Somewhere Over the Rainbow."

As Chantal played, Sophie sat cross-legged on the floor and hummed the melody. Papa sat on the daybed and smiled, letting his eyes turn to slits. Chantal loved the pleasure and comfort people drew from music.

By the time she played the last chorus, Papa was fast asleep, his eyelids already twitching in a dream. Sophie stretched out too, after giving her niece a kiss on the cheek.

Chantal was left wide awake, the ukulele still in her hands. She should go to bed, she really should. But instead, a plan formed in her mind. An excellent plan inspired by the music.

She waited patiently. As soon as Sophie's snoring matched the intensity of Papa's, Chantal got up and took her ukulele. Through the living room she tiptoed, her eyes on her sleeping father.

Sorry, Papa. When destiny calls, you have to answer.

She made no noise as she opened and closed the door. No noise as she swooshed down the six flights of stairs and flew into the night, alone.

13

ANOTHER REALM, ANOTHER WORLD

T he river was still and dark, waiting. Chantal had never been out at night by herself before. Not in Paris. She climbed down to the embankment and sat as close to the water as she dared.

She placed her fingers into position on the ukulele's neck and strummed the first chord to "Somewhere Over the Rainbow." The chord winged over the water, farther and farther, then vanished.

No sound came in reply, not from the water or anywhere near the river.

Chantal strummed the chord again and followed it up with the second chord. She listened, her heart a bundle of nervous hope.

Nothing.

"If you're out there," she said to the river, to the night, "now is the time to make yourself known."

Chantal played the two chords again.

In the distance, the water sloshed.

Then it happened.

The water rippled. A large black back broke through the surface.

"Grrrrrooool-th-th-th!" echoed off the stone walls.

Chantal laughed from fright and amazement and joy.

The creature swam closer to Chantal, and its face appeared. Two black eyes set far apart. A long and bumpy snout . . . or nose—she didn't know what to call it. She felt giddy, as light as air.

The creature's long body arced back from its forehead. She had been right: It *was* a whale. Its fins were churning the water on either side of its body, creating inky whirlpools in the dead of night. The whale was treading water.

Was she dreaming?

Chantal closed her eyes and opened them again. The whale remained absolutely and undeniably there. She propped her ukulele against a tree and crawled even closer to the massive creature. Her stomach whirled as though she were on a Ferris wheel.

"So you're the one who's been eating our salmon," she said.

"Grrrrrooool-th-th-th!"

The whale swam up to the riverbank as if to approach her.

Chantal eased back. The fear was sharp and searing, the same fear she always had near the water.

The whale blew out a jet spray and purred like a giant cat. It then made a *moo* like that of a cow. What a strange animal!

Chantal smiled and relaxed. She scooted forward again.

"Yeeeeooooooowwwwwl," said the whale. It followed the sound with a pattern of five clicks.

"I'll come even closer if you promise not to eat me."

The whale seemed to nod its head in the water. Or was it Chantal's imagination?

No. She was certain it nodded.

She crept closer.

Closer.

Could she touch it? Should she?

She only needed to extend her arm and . . .

No, she pulled back, disappointed with herself because she wanted to be brave. She reached out again and . . .

She touched it! She touched the whale! Just for a second, but she had actually touched it. She tried again. This time a bit longer. She ran her hand along its back, the wet part she could reach that was exposed to the air.

It felt like magic, like happiness. Cold and true and alive. The whale's skin was so textured and rutted, her fingers couldn't leave it alone.

There she was, petting a giant creature from the sea. If only Mama could see her now.

Chantal's fingertips glided across the whale's rough skin. In response, the whale made a soft chirping noise. Encouraged, she used both hands. She raced them across the back of the floating whale and laughed.

"Grrrrooool-th-th-th!"

Was she tickling the whale? It sloshed and splattered, submerging, only an inch or two, before coming back up. This time Chantal could see its two blowholes. She didn't dare touch them. Something about the blowholes seemed too intimate.

She extended her hand, and with a more delicate touch than before, stroked the creature's snout or nose. Its smell was strong now, a smell of low tide, seaweed, and clam shells.

Was the whale a girl or a boy? She knew, almost without hesitation, that it was a boy. She didn't know how she knew, yet she did.

The creature shuddered softly as she ran her hand over his bumps and knobs and small domes like buttons.

He wasn't exactly warm to the touch. It wasn't like placing your hand on a person and feeling the warmth rise. Nor was he cold. He just *was*.

She studied his eyes, like two distant planets—Saturn to be exact, aquamarine rings around a central black orb. They were eyes that blinked with lids as thick as elephant skin. Eyes that looked at her.

She stared at the eyes, and the eyes stared back.

She winked and one eye winked back.

Chantal imagined what the whale might be thinking. *Where am I? Who is this girl? Why am I here?*

With her hand still on the whale, it was almost as though she could sense the creature's fear. How strange. *If one of us should be afraid,* she thought, *it should be me.*

But Chantal wasn't afraid. Not anymore. She kept her hand on the whale's head and said, "Where do you come from?"

"Grrrrroooooooom," went the whale.

"That is a place I'm unfamiliar with."

"Chchchchch."

"You are far from the sea. Why are you here?"

"Krewoif . . . Eu, ech, ech, ech . . . oewirwo."

The whale spoke a language from the ancient

beginnings of the Earth. From a primordial place, beyond the wall of time.

"Show me the rest of you."

With that, the creature drifted away from her hand and into the thick of the river. He snorted several times through his blowholes, and with a plosive *whoosh!* he filled his lungs, dove, and kicked up his tail fin into the air.

From what Chantal could tell, the whale was about twenty feet long. Big to her, but small for a whale.

A side fin banded in white came up in a wave, and then the creature faded below the depths. Darkness and water engulfed him.

Chantal gulped in air and held her breath, as though she'd been the one who just dove underwater, disappearing into another realm, another world.

14

LE GRAND JOUR

Chantal said good-bye to what was hiding in the river, not for always, she hoped. She mounted the stone steps up to the quay. It was absolutely necessary to return to bed before Papa or Aunt Sophie woke up and found her gone. There was enough trouble going around without them having to worry about her.

Her heart, so filled with her magical encounter, barely noticed the six-floor climb to the apartment. She took off her shoes, snuck in (avoiding the spots where she knew the floorboards creaked), undressed, slipped into her flannel pajamas, and snuggled into her bed.

She fell asleep almost immediately.

The white nightmare did not come for her.

Hours later, in the early daylight, she was awakened by Papa's voice: *"Cherie!* Wake up. I have good news. We didn't tell you last night, in case it didn't happen, but I can tell you now—"

"They're coming?" Chantal asked, her eyes blinking open.

"No," Papa said. "Better . . . *C'est le Grand Jour*—the Big Day. They're already here!"

Chantal leaped from her bed. Her chest stretched as wide as the sky. The feeling was five Christmas mornings plus ten New Year's Eves.

She rushed to the window to see the Allies. Their soldiers. Their jeeps. Their tanks. Their flags.

But there was nothing. Only the empty quay below her window, and beyond that the green Seine and the buildings looking like wedding cakes.

"Where are they?"

Papa came up behind her and held her tight. He bent down. She could feel his breath at her ear.

"They landed at Normandy, while you were sleeping."

Although it was only a whisper, the power it packed was that of thunder.

So it was true! She swung around and hugged Papa, who lifted her off her feet.

In the kitchen, Aunt Sophie was fiddling with the radio's knob. She turned, her smile brighter than pure sunshine.

With the eggs that didn't go into last night's salmon quiche, Papa cooked up an omelette. They all listened to the broadcast of the BBC.

The invasion was massive.

The Allies had bombarded Calais, Le Havre, Dunkirk.

Paratroopers had landed everywhere.

The Allies were attacking from the air . . . and by the sea.

The attack was called "a new phase in the offensive."

The news was so exciting, Chantal could barely eat her omelette as she listened to the radio. She looked at the calendar on the wall. *Le Grand Jour.* D-day. The date was June sixth.

After breakfast, Aunt Sophie suggested they go out for a walk. She was too thrilled by the news to stay indoors.

"But there's school," Chantal objected.

Sophie waved away the suggestion. "Nonsense. Nobody goes to school on a day like this. How could you concentrate?"

She had a point.

"What about you?" Sophie said to Papa. "Do you have school?"

Soon, the three of them were out the door, dashing down the six flights of stairs.

Chantal was carrying her mother's ukulele.

In the morning's excitement, she had forgotten to tell Papa and Aunt Sophie about the whale. But was that entirely true? It was more that she didn't know *how* to tell them. After all, she'd left the apartment under the cover of darkness, without a word to anyone. How could she tell them about the whale without getting herself into trouble?

Besides, Chantal feared she would be laughed at again. They hadn't believed her before. Nobody had. Why would they believe her now?

The quay was busier than usual. The sun was high and a soft wind stirred. Still, it was more than the fine weather that had drawn people out of their homes. They'd heard the news and were milling about in a state of rapture. The Allies had landed! Soon the French would be free!

They walked along the quay, high above the river. Chantal kept glancing down into the water, scanning for signs of the whale. The river flowed as steadily as usual without any disturbance from below. Would the whale show himself if she played him another song?

On Pont Saint-Louis, they stopped to watch the

painter on the bridge. A typical riverbank scene was underway. Chantal approached the canvas and looked closely at the brushstrokes. There seemed to be an added feature to the landscape—a smudge, a long and dark shape swimming in the river.

Had the painter seen the whale too?

A feeling soared inside her until she couldn't hold it back any longer. "Can we go down to the river?" she asked. "I have something to show you."

Papa and Aunt Sophie eyed her dubiously.

"Please? It will only take a minute."

Thanks to the general good mood, nobody objected. The three of them turned around and made their way down to the river. They came to the spot where Chantal and Papa usually fished.

The Seine flowed lazily past their feet, the water all green and murky. Nothing stirring in its depths, or so it seemed.

Chantal sat down on the stones and strummed a C major on the ukulele.

She strummed it again and waited.

"What are you doing?" Papa asked.

"*Shhh.* We have to be quiet and patient."

Chantal strummed the next chord: E minor.

When nothing happened, she began to play "Somewhere Over the Rainbow" in its entirety.

With all the chord changes, it wasn't an easy song to play, but if she let her mind go and didn't focus too hard, her hands seemed to take over from her thoughts, and the music came in a flow.

Chantal was nearing the end of the song when she heard the first rumble. Electrified, she turned to her father and aunt.

"Did you hear that?" she asked.

Papa and Sophie nodded. Yes, they'd heard it.

Chantal kept playing the ukulele.

Seconds later, a dark shape broke through the surface of the water in a hiss of splashes and vapor. Chantal stopped playing and looked up to her father and aunt again.

Sophie cupped a hand over her mouth. "Wow! That is . . . that is . . ."

"Incredible," said Papa, beaming with joy. The whale could be clearly seen now, paddling and sloshing. "He swam from the English Channel all the way up the Seine!"

"I told you," Chantal said with humor and not in a mean way. She was relieved that everyone would stop thinking she invented silly, hopeful stories.

She looked at the whale again. Her triumph. In the daylight, he was bigger than she remembered. Long and deep blue, almost black, with white chevrons striping his fins. He balanced in the river, vibrating with excitement, as if he'd been politely waiting underwater for Chantal to finish the song.

Did he remember her?

She scooted down to the water's edge, forgetting to be afraid.

"Careful," Papa said from behind her.

"Oh, let her be," said Sophie.

Chantal stretched out her hand and touched the whale's nose. He shivered with pleasure and let out a few *wops*.

"Did you like the song?" she asked.

The whale nodded.

"Would you like to hear another?"

The whale nodded again.

"I can't believe my eyes," Sophie said.

As Chantal played a slow, haunting song, the whale sang to her ukulele. His singing was like ribbons of sound unfurling. A pure joy. Certainly he was inventing his own lyrics, much like Papa invented his dishes. Chantal didn't mind, not one bit.

The next song she chose was a fast, rollicking number, a piece of music her mother had liked to play at parties. The whale squealed with delight and rolled onto his back. He swam for a moment like this, upside down, then flipped over again and paddled in a circle in front of her.

Chantal kept playing. Tapping her foot to the beat. Smiling and laughing all the while.

Papa and Sophie began clapping. When Chantal glanced around to meet their eyes, she noticed a crowd had gathered on the quay above them. People, young and old, were watching the whale with fascination. Among them was a German soldier.

"What is it?" someone asked.

"Where did it come from?"

"It's a miracle!"

And Chantal felt it *was* a miracle. Her playing the ukulele on a warm summer day. The whale rolling and frolicking in the water. Was it a coincidence that he'd appeared just as the Allies landed? Of course not. The whale was a sign of good luck. A blessing.

The whale meant the war would be over soon.

15

WHAT'S IN A NAME?

The whale submerged himself again, probably in search of lunch. Chantal, Papa, and Aunt Sophie climbed up to the quay to talk with the curious crowd.

Chantal answered their questions as best as she could—how she'd first heard the whale three nights ago, then saw him the next. How she touched his back and they became friends. How she was sure the whale was a boy.

"So what's his name?" a woman asked.

This question stumped Chantal. So far, the whale had just been "the whale." But the woman was right. The whale should have a name.

"I'll tell you tomorrow," she promised.

At home, Chantal, Papa, and Aunt Sophie sat again in the kitchen to listen to the next BBC broadcast. There were more details about the Allied invasion, or "D-day" as it was now called.

More than four thousand ships had crossed the English Channel to France.

And eleven thousand airplanes.

Eleven thousand airplanes?

The number staggered Chantal. She was surprised, and apparently so were the Germans, Winston Churchill said. Or maybe it was the radio announcer only quoting Winston Churchill. It was difficult for Chantal to tell the difference.

The invasion was huge, and being led by an American named General Eisenhower. The Allies were fighting the Germans on the beaches. Massive airborne landings had happened behind enemy lines—the news was even more promising than it had been that morning!

When the radio said that Churchill's speech was

cheered in Parliament, Chantal, Papa, and Aunt Sophie, in their tiny makeshift kitchen, behind those enemy lines, also cheered.

That night in bed, Chantal's thoughts returned to the whale. What should she name him?

Julien? Michel? Jean-Christophe?

Such names were far too ordinary for a miraculous whale. She needed a name that was powerful, something significant.

Winston Churchill? General Eisenhower?

She didn't like these names.

What about Franklin Roosevelt? The president of the United States. The Americans had crossed the entire Atlantic to save France, and now they were fighting on the beaches of Normandy.

The president's name spoke to Chantal. From Aunt Sophie she'd learned that Roosevelt was originally a Dutch name that meant "field of roses."

It reminded her of a sunny afternoon with Mama in the countryside. Just the two of them. They were talking and laughing, picking wild blackberries, when they came upon a field of roses—red, white, and pink flowers as far as the eye could see. They fell silent, in loving harmony with nature's beauty. Chantal could still feel the squeeze of her mother's hand as they gazed in awe, the delicious scent swimming all around them, caressing their faces.

A field of roses is a peaceful place.

A field of roses is somewhere people might go to forget about the war.

She had hit upon the right name. Though Franklin Roosevelt was rather a long name for a small whale, so she shortened it to Franklin.

16

VERY SPECIAL FERRY

After school the next day, Chantal was outside with her ukulele by the Seine. The crowd was three times bigger than the day before and had attracted the attention of not one but two German soldiers. They stood guard with their guns, keeping a close eye.

Instead of worrying about the soldiers, Chantal kissed Odette's cheeks, or rather the air around them. Odette had brought her blue diamond kite with a tail of red ribbon. The kite was in sad shape, held together by bits of wire. Odette had crashed it many times.

Along with her friend, Chantal greeted most of her classmates.

"Where is he?" they asked.

Other people in the crowd starting asking too. Everyone wanted to see Chantal's whale, for that's what they were calling him. The people who didn't know her called him "The Little Girl's Whale."

"His name is Franklin," she said to the crowd before sitting down with her ukulele to play a song. On the instrument's neck, her hand automatically formed the first chord of "Somewhere Over the Rainbow," the song that had summoned the great creature the day before.

But she stopped herself. The same song would be boring, wouldn't it? Chantal hated repetitiveness, which was probably why she disliked school. She decided to play another tune, George Gershwin's "I Got Rhythm," and she played it with all the soul and swing she could muster.

Most of the people who were waiting for Franklin to surface turned to one another and began to dance. Those who couldn't dance or find a partner swayed softly to the music.

Minutes later, Franklin burst from the depths of the Seine. The crowd cheered. Chantal couldn't remember the last time anybody had cheered for anything.

She scooted down to the water's edge and stroked

Franklin's nose. He purred and croaked and made his clicking sounds.

For the rest of the day, they invented games together. Chantal played the ukulele and Franklin sang along. She ran up and down the embankment and he swam after her. She threw her hands in the air and he shot a great spout of water upward.

At one point, Chantal borrowed Odette's kite. She tied the kite to a life preserver from a nearby boat and threw the preserver in the water. Franklin pushed the preserver up and down the Seine between Pont de la Tournelle and Pont Saint-Louis. For the first time in history, a whale was flying a kite.

As the afternoon came to an end, Odette announced that she would like to take her kite back home. She climbed Pont de la Tournelle to intercept it before Franklin made another circuit between the two bridges. She vaulted the parapet and reached out her hand. Unfortunately, as always, she was clumsy. Her foot slipped and into the water she went.

"Au secours!" she cried. (Help!)

The crowd grew frantic. Several men pulled off their shoes, preparing to dive into the river. But Franklin was already there, heading straight for Odette.

"Au secours!" she cried.

Chantal was anxious. Would he bite Odette? Swim over her, push her under? After all, Franklin was a whale, massive and wild and swimming fast. Chantal held her breath, hoping . . . which was when he submerged, came up under Odette, and bore her out of the water. Chantal was so proud: One friend was rescuing the other! The crowd applauded, and Odette smiled at her good fortune, stretching out her arms as though to catch their joy, her wet red hair shining in the sun.

"*Magnifique!*" cried someone. (Magnificent!)

It certainly is, Chantal thought. Franklin was a very special whale.

The very special whale proceeded to take Odette on a ride from one side of the river to the other. Hence, a new game was born. Some children straddled Franklin as though he were a horse. Others sat cross-legged or knelt. The brave ones rode him standing up as you would a surfboard.

As for the adults, none took a ride on Franklin that day because there were too many children ahead of them in line.

"What about you, Chantal?" said Odette. "Don't you want to ride him?"

Chantal had dreaded the question. While she enjoyed seeing the other children climb onto Franklin's back, she didn't dare do so herself. It seemed a giant step, from the dry riverbank to a slippery whale, only inches above the treacherous water.

"I wouldn't want to take anyone's turn," she said, trying to save face. "I can ride him anytime."

17

WISHES AND FISH

The strip of embankment between Pont de la Tournelle and Pont Saint-Louis became like a family room where Parisians met. The whale had changed the world. At least their world. And he had given Chantal a new sense of purpose.

Each day after school, she and Odette drew small tickets on a piece of paper and cut them away with a pair of scissors. Whenever someone wanted to see Franklin up close (one ticket), or ride him across the Seine (two tickets), Odette would collect the fare while

Chantal supervised the interaction each person had with Franklin.

The cost of a ticket was a positive comment or a wish. In this way, Chantal and Odette distracted everyone from worrying about the Allies and when they might break through the enemy lines to liberate the rest of France.

People might say: "What a lovely day it is today" (even if it was cloudy), or "You are as kind and giving as your mother," or "I like the tickle of grass on my feet," or "I wish I had a cup of coffee. Coffee was one of the finest things," or "Oysters were delicious," and so forth.

But for the most part, people wished for the war to end.

While Chantal and Odette "sold" their tickets, the painter captured the scenes. A whale in Paris! Day after day he sat at his easel, painting Franklin playing his games. Soon he had a small collection of paintings that he tried to sell to the people waiting in line. He wasn't very successful at it, because no one had money to spare.

It was a shame, Chantal thought. She found the paintings to be splendid, full of depth and raw emotion, especially *The Magnificent Rescue of Odette*. She was impressed by the way the painter had captured her friend's essence, her surprise and elation at being saved.

Just a few strokes of color conveyed more than a photograph could. She had faith that one day the painter would be discovered and appreciated.

When school officially ended and the summer holidays began, Chantal and Odette spent entire days with Franklin. The games were a serious operation, and they had to oversee each stage—orderly lines, no pushing, regular breaks for Franklin. It was a job neither of them could do alone. The cooperation strengthened their friendship. Despite the war, this summer promised to be the best holiday of all time.

But the war was there all the same. German eyes watched them from both sides of the river. Chantal was glad the soldiers kept their distance and didn't intervene. None of them had asked to ride Franklin.

One morning, Professor Petit appeared in line, as though he already missed his pupils in the classroom.

"*Bonjour,*" he said, tipping his hat to Chantal as he approached.

"*Bonjour, Maître.*"

"I've come to take a look at your whale."

"His name is Franklin."

Professor Petit went on about what a well-suited name Franklin was for a whale and how Chantal was doing such a good job sharing him with the rest of the city. She felt the professor was being too nice to her, babying her, and she wondered why.

"Do you still think I'm a silly girl?" she asked.

His ears grew so red, they were almost purple. "No. I never thought that. I only said it to protect you. You are not silly. Not at all."

She supposed he was telling the truth. Still, "silly" had been the first word that had occurred to him when Private Schröder had come into the classroom to question Chantal. Some part of the word must have been sincere.

Professor Petit moved up in the line. "I knew you were covering for"—he lowered his voice—"Odette, when she broke the Easter eggs. She's not as graceful as she'd like to be."

Chantal fought back a smile. Her teacher was more perceptive than she'd assumed . . . and kinder.

He gestured toward Franklin. "The whale makes sounds, yes?"

Chantal nodded.

"Do you understand the sounds?"

The question surprised her. No one had asked her that before.

"No, monsieur. Not yet."

Professor Petit seemed to appreciate the "not yet," as

if he, too, had been studying Franklin's secret language. Chantal had thought she was the only one.

She related to the professor what she had learned. A pattern of five evenly spaced clicks meant either *Yes, please* or *Now*. High-frequency screams indicated disagreement. (Franklin often had his own ideas and couldn't be dissuaded.) A *wop* sound was sometimes a question mark and sometimes an exclamation point. A warble was laughter.

Other sounds were more difficult to categorize, though she tried. There were snorts, growls, screeches, buzzes, chirrups, purrs, hisses, trumpets, tweets, booms, and a trilling sort of frimple. Chantal would need more time to understand what these meant.

Professor Petit was impressed. And he wasn't the only one she was impressing these days. Her alliance with Franklin made her appear more mysterious and more interesting than she knew she was. Chantal was the girl who'd discovered a whale, a creature from another realm. People greeted her wherever she went. She was a household name. Even the painter offered to paint her portrait, which Chantal declined.

"Why?" quizzed Odette.

"Because," Chantal said. "I'd feel ridiculous sitting there for hours."

The truth was, her sudden fame confused her. She was

delighted with the extra attention, but it also filled her with dread. Both Papa and Aunt Sophie had told her not to stand out. She was supposed to blend in and be invisible. In times of war, drawing attention was dangerous.

Sure enough, Papa grew concerned. "I don't like how you spend your days, entertaining everyone," he said, when Chantal came home one evening. He was at the sink, washing a few potatoes. "You used to be a serious girl."

"Franklin gives people hope, Papa. Isn't that serious?"

He answered with a frown. "Not as serious as food. You never go fishing with me anymore."

It was true. Papa had taken to fishing alone off the Square du Vert-Galant, a triangle jutting out into the Seine. He, the fisherman, hoped to catch the salmon before Franklin, the fisherwhale, gobbled them up. But in the week following Franklin's arrival, Papa had only managed to catch a small bucketful of palm-sized bream and two silvery cods.

"Please, Papa," Chantal said. "It's the summer holiday."

"Yes, *cherie*. But it's also war. The German soldiers on the quay are keeping an eye on you. Have you forgotten what happened at school?"

No, she hadn't forgotten. But Franklin wasn't a threat to the Germans. Enemy maneuvers? He was just a whale.

"Why can't you be happy for me?" she asked.

Hearing these words, Papa's face changed. He rinsed his hands and dried them on a towel before turning to Chantal, his arms opened wide. "Come here. Of course I'm happy for you."

Chantal rushed toward him and buried her head in his chest. She breathed him in. How she loved Papa's smell. Hints of tobacco and leather mixed with river tang and the crumble of dark earth.

But when they let go and she looked up, the frown was there again. He wasn't happy. Not happy at all. What was he not telling her?

The next day brought the kind of unpleasant surprise Papa had warned her about. Major Klaus Wölfflin appeared on the quay.

Major Klaus Wölfflin was one of the top German officers assigned to Paris. Chantal had never seen him, yet she'd heard of him. He was feared and hated.

The people in line at the quay began to whisper his name, and that's when Chantal noticed him observing her and Franklin from a distance. Then she saw him coming down the stone steps. Heard the *Schomp! Bluck!* of his boots.

She busied herself with Franklin and a child that wanted a ride, hoping the major would pass her by.

"Mademoiselle Duprey."

The raspy voice came from behind her. Chantal drew in a breath and turned.

Immediately she understood why Major Wölfflin was so feared. He looked as pale as a waxwork, though hard-eyed, like a figure out of a dark carnival.

"So," Major Wölfflin said. "This is your *submarine*?"

Chantal swallowed. Was he making a joke?

"It's a whale, monsieur," she said in a voice that was barely audible.

"Oh yes. Thank you for clarifying that. A whale named Franklin."

Chantal nodded, too afraid to speak.

"Why have you not named him Gustav? Or Heinrich? Or Adolf? Or Klaus?" Major Klaus Wölfflin asked.

Again, Chantal was at a loss for words.

A grin flashed on the major's fleshy lips. "Don't worry," he said. "I find it humorous that the great President Roosevelt has been reduced to a fish."

He's not a fish, Chantal wanted to say. *He's a mammal.* But she kept that thought to herself.

Franklin seemed to disagree with the major too. As if offended, he flapped his tail in the water, causing a small wave to wash over the embankment.

Startled, Major Wölfflin stumbled backward, almost tripping over a child who'd been waiting for a ride. The major patted down his uniform, turned on his heel, and made his way toward the steps leading up to the quay.

Chantal, along with everyone else on the embankment, sighed with relief.

She came home that night to find Aunt Sophie fiddling with the knobs of the radio in preparation for the BBC's broadcast. Aunt Sophie was now temporarily living with the Duprey family. Ever since the Allies had landed in Normandy, that part of the country was a war zone. It was impossible for her to return to Honfleur.

Papa didn't seem thrilled with Sophie's constant presence, but Chantal did her best to show him how much she loved having her aunt around.

The three of them huddled around the radio.

Astonishing news from the French capital! A whale has been sighted. . . . That's right, a whale in the Seine! Under the noses of the Nazis, he swam all the way from the English Channel to the steps of Notre Dame. Is he leading the way for the Allies? Who knows. All this broadcaster can say is—wonders never cease!

A grin broke out on Chantal's face, wide and joyful. Sophie, in her enthusiasm, did a little dance right there in the kitchen.

Papa, though, remained silent, still dubious of Chantal and her marine friend. He was looking agitated, worried even. Why was he so glum?

The Allies would arrive in Paris any day now.

The war was almost over.

Right?

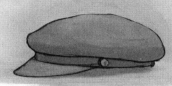

18

RAIN

One afternoon, it began raining. A soft summer rain. At first Chantal went outside as usual to play with Franklin. A bit of rain wasn't going to dissuade her or most of her fellow Parisians from seeing the whale. In their slickers, Odette and Chantal kept selling tickets.

But the sky over the Seine remained low and dark, day after day. Soon the rain was only pouring and never plopping. Fewer people came to see Franklin. The happiness he'd brought to Paris was now hidden behind a veil of gray.

It rained and rained. Puddles became small lakes. The streets flooded into marshes. People broke down crates to make footbridges to get to their front doors. It rained so much, Chantal was in fear of drowning each time she went outside. She spent more of her time watching Franklin from her window, six stories up. His swimming was restricted to floating, and then only in the stretch of river directly below her apartment building. As if he was waiting for her.

Did he miss being with her as much as she missed being with him?

Whenever there was a break in the weather, she raced down to the Seine to pay her friend a visit, and each time Franklin seemed to temporarily revive.

Still, it was not like before.

At night in the dark, Chantal reached for Mama. All she felt was a hole where her mother used to be. Too often, the white nightmare returned. In the eerie quiet of her loneliest dream, the white tendrils rose out of the blanket of mist and swirled around her ankles.

An unexpected storm lashed across the English Channel, lasting three days. The rain in Paris had only been the opening notes of a savage tempest.

Chantal, Papa, and Aunt Sophie sat in the kitchen listening to the secret radio. The news was bad. About eight hundred Allied ships, bringing fresh supplies and troops, had been lost in the storm and sent to the bottom of the sea.

"Eight hundred!" cried Chantal. She thought of all the poor drowning men on their way to help those who'd already landed weeks ago, the men who never arrived in Paris.

Where were they?

Aunt Sophie explained the situation. Although the Allies had succeeded in storming the beaches, they were now mired in a section of Normandy called the *bocage*, or hedgerows, filled with briars and thick, thorny brush as high as a man's head. The giant hedges were meant to define properties and protect livestock. But now they were protecting the Germans and choking the Allies.

German strongholds were everywhere. Concrete bunkers. Ammunition depots. Guns and grenades in relentless accumulation.

The Allies were sitting ducks.

19

HOMESICK

After the rains, the sky cleared, and people gathered again by the banks of the Seine with the hopes of Franklin ferrying them across.

Chantal was there, of course, though not Odette. Chantal waited for her friend until the crowd grew impatient. With no help from Odette, she let a boy climb on the whale's back.

But Franklin didn't cross the river.

"What's wrong?" she asked, stroking his head.

No nod. Not even a squeak.

This worried Chantal. Was Franklin finished play-ing the ferry game? She sent the boy away and helped a small girl shimmy up onto the whale's back. Again, Franklin didn't budge. He just floated there, sullen and disinterested, looking far off into the distance, as if he didn't want to see the people who wanted to see him.

Or perhaps as if he were searching for something that was no longer there.

Chantal tried to imagine his unusual journey. How one day he'd taken a wrong turn chasing a school of salmon. How he'd noticed too late that he was alone and his family was no longer with him. How he'd kept swim-ming in an effort to find his pod. How he'd only gotten farther and farther away.

She put her hands on his nose and understood: Franklin was homesick.

"C'mon, girl," a man in line said. "Tell him to take us across."

"Yes! He's *your* whale," another chimed in. "Tell him to do as he's told!"

Chantal didn't want to force Franklin to do something against his will. "He's not our slave," she said.

The people grew angry with her. The least he could do was entertain them, they said. After all, he was eating all the fish in the Seine.

Chantal petted Franklin. "They don't mean any harm."

Franklin grunted and whistled.

"They just want to have fun," she said.

Franklin let out two chirps, a neigh, and a long noise between a hoot and a frimple. Chantal took this to mean that he didn't agree.

She wanted to embrace him and assure him that everything would be all right, but she sensed his intelligence, his ability to discern deception. It was better to be honest with him. Be a true friend.

"They're acting mean because they're tired of the war," she said. "But it's not your fault, Franklin. Not your fault."

2⦿

BLACKMAILED BY HUNGER

Food became very scarce in Paris. There hadn't been much to go around since the beginning of the war, but after D-day there was even less. Vegetables, grains, and meats had trouble reaching the capital, because many bridges over the Seine north of Paris had been destroyed.

The bombing had been an Allied tactical maneuver to make it more difficult for the Germans to retreat and send reinforcements. Unfortunately, destroying the bridges had other effects: The fertile farms in Normandy could no longer transport their products to Paris.

And where were the Allies? Were the Germans winning?

In every house and on every street corner, there was worry. Ration tickets were still handed out to those who had their papers, but what good were coupons when there was no food in the shops?

The only place where business thrived was the black market. Butter cost as much as thirty-one francs an ounce, according to Aunt Sophie.

A new main course emerged in French cuisine—*Rat Grillé*. Rat catchers were charging hefty prices for their services. These men ventured into the sewers where the black plague was still rumored to be found.

Even the mice stopped scampering in the walls.

Paris was starving.

In the Duprey kitchen, Chantal, Papa, and Aunt Sophie ate the last of what remained in the cool box: some scraps of cod and a few old salmon skins.

"Are there any oats left?" asked Chantal. She opened the pantry to the right of the stove. There were only two sacks of rice and one of dried kidney beans. A year ago, Papa had successfully hidden a small barrel of potatoes and apples in the basement of the apartment building. A barrel that now lived in their kitchen.

They were halfway through that.

"Let's go out and fish tonight," suggested Chantal.

Papa sighed. "What do you think I've been doing? There aren't any fish left!"

His temper upset Chantal. "It's not Franklin's fault."

Sophie stood by the window and pointed at the whale coasting back and forth. "But it is, *ma chou*. Who else is eating our fish?"

Chantal didn't want to admit it out loud, but she knew they were right.

Papa put his hands on her shoulders. "We may have to think about sending Franklin away."

Chantal stamped her foot. "No!"

How could her father even suggest that? You can't send a friend away. Even if he eats your fish.

"We don't have a choice," Papa said. "Franklin doesn't belong here."

"He has as much right to be here as we do."

Papa grumbled, unable to reply. Chantal thought about their dilemma. Even if Franklin were to be sent away, how would something like that be accomplished? He wasn't like a dog you take to the woods and release. She knew that as long as she stayed in Paris, the whale wasn't going anywhere.

"But, *ma chou*," Aunt Sophie said, "don't you think he deserves to go home?"

With this, Chantal could only agree. She knew how sad he'd become. What was best for them might also be best for Franklin.

21

FATHER MAURICE, MOTHER NATURE II

*A*fter a week of not eating more than a handful of food each day, Chantal learned that hunger was akin to holding her breath. She could tolerate it, though not for long. Remembering what Papa and Aunt Sophie had said about Franklin eating their fish, she tried to eat as little as possible. But eventually, she had to put something in her mouth, even if it was only the tiniest bite of food—a scrap of bread, a cold potato, half a brown pear, the crust left on a piece of cheese.

Chantal chewed each nibble slowly until there was

nothing left to chew. Then she sucked on the paste for as long as possible, before it melted and slid down her throat.

One day, Chantal returned to the gardens behind Notre Dame. If she lent a hand as before, maybe Father Maurice would give her a carrot or two.

Dread crept into her step as she walked. Chantal feared that Father Maurice would be angry with her for not showing up sooner. It had been so long since she last helped with the harvesting and weeding. She'd felt too embarrassed to go back after everyone had laughed at her about the submarine.

Her heart sank when she arrived: The torrential rains had turned the Garden of Eden into a ransacked swamp. There were at least a hundred people crouched in the mud, pulling up roots and digging in the dirt.

"Well, look who it is," said Father Maurice, handing her a spade and a burlap sack.

Chantal didn't know whether he was being sarcastic or not. She took the spade and the sack and asked what she could do.

"Help us clean up," he said. "The plots are ruined. If you happen to find any leftovers buried in the mud, you can keep them."

Chantal looked at the volunteers already at work. Many faces she didn't recognize. The faces of spies?

She wondered which one of them had reported her submarine to the Germans.

She chose an uncrowded corner, squatted in the mud, and started to separate rotten branches from edible leaves, trash from treasure.

"Don't touch that," an angry voice snapped. "It's *my* area."

Chantal shrugged and moved farther down the line. Just as she was about to get to work, someone else interrupted her. "Not here. Whatever's here is mine."

Up and down the rows she went, the slippery earth slurping at her feet, searching for anyone who would allow her to pick through the rubbish of plants. Each time she was either pushed aside or asked to leave.

"What is *she* doing here?" a woman asked, pointing at Chantal with a pitchfork.

Gardeners nearby glanced up from their work. Their tired, hungry eyes held a cruel look.

"I'm sorry," Chantal said to all of them, as sincerely as possible. "I'm sorry I haven't come around lately to help."

"You were too busy with your whale, weren't you?" a man said.

It was a mean question that begged no reply.

"Why don't you go back to him and see if he can spare a morsel," said someone else Chantal didn't know. "He eats well enough, doesn't he?"

Chantal stood there, not knowing what to say. Where was Father Maurice? She looked around for a sympathetic face. There was none.

"The famine isn't Franklin's fault," she said. "You shouldn't blame him."

"Why not?" came another anonymous voice.

Chantal understood why they were upset. Everyone was hungry. But anger had never fed anyone.

"He made you happy, remember?" she said. "Isn't that worth something?" She smiled as a sign of goodwill, but as she smiled she realized: Goodwill had never fed anyone either.

"Happiness is worthless when you're starving!" a man shouted.

Roars of approval followed this statement.

Things happened fast after that, as though a spell had been broken.

Rough, discordant voices broke out:

"We are hungry because of the whale."

"He's eating our fish when we should be eating him!"

"Let's get that greedy gobbler!"

"No," Chantal shouted, dropping her spade and sack. "No!"

Nobody paid any attention to her.

"He can feed *us* for a change."

"We won't go hungry tonight!"

"Whale steaks."

"Blubber soup!"

"We must save ourselves!"

"*Allez!* Let's go!"

The gardeners, a glowing fury in their eyes, grabbed any tool they could find—hoes, pickaxes, rakes, shovels—and hastened toward the Seine. Chantal ran fast, slipping between them and surging ahead.

She reached the embankment first and found Franklin basking in a ray of sun, dozing in tranquility.

"Swim!" Chantal called. "Swim away, now!"

Franklin opened one of his black eyes and then the other. He seemed to understand the urgency of the situation. Just as the angry crowd came down the stone steps, Franklin eased away from the bank into the center of the river. There he submerged, leaving behind a boiling jumble of bubbles.

The crowd rushed forward, yelling.

"Get him!"

They threw their tools into the bubbles as though chucking spears.

Splash! and *Splonk!* went the iron tools into the water.

Chantal was about to throw herself into the Seine in a last attempt to protect Franklin, when . . .

A pistol *CRACK!* ripped through the air.

22

A HEAVY ARM

Major Klaus Wölfflin stood on the quay, his pistol pointed at the sky, a gunpowder cloud drifting away from its barrel. Soldiers quickly flanked him.

"Nobody move," he called down.

Move? Chantal thought. She could barely breathe.

Everyone on the embankment froze and waited for Major Wölfflin to descend the stone stairs. His soldiers shouldered together and inched down behind him.

"The first person to lift a hand against that whale will be shot," Major Wölfflin said, pushing through the crowd that had gathered. Some of them were the gardeners, still holding the tools they hadn't flung into the water. Others were bystanders who'd approached from the sides of the embankment and beneath the bridge to see who had fired the shot.

Chantal felt reassured when she noticed Aunt Sophie among them. Sophie edged through the bodies until she was standing directly behind Chantal, her hands firmly on her niece's shoulders.

"Out of my way," said Major Wölfflin as he continued to push toward the river. "You, girl. Step forward!"

He burned his gaze directly at Chantal. She could feel her aunt's hands turning into steel claws.

"Don't ignore me. I said, come here!" The major gestured to one of the soldiers flanking him.

The soldier snapped to action and stepped up to Sophie. "Let the child go."

Sophie didn't budge.

Up came a rifle butt as quick as a flash. It slammed into Sophie's side. Chantal felt her collapse to the ground behind her.

She whipped around. "Aunt Sophie!" Thunderstorms exploded in her mind and gushed into her balled fists. The soldier grabbed her by the arm and yanked her closer to the major.

"Face me," said Major Wölfflin.

Chantal was shoved and manhandled to face the major. Suddenly the entire world shrunk to him and her. She told herself not to flinch.

"So we meet again," he said, smiling.

A "Grrrrroool-th-th-th!" sounded from the river. Like everyone else, Chantal turned to find that Franklin had resurfaced.

Major Wölfflin glanced from Chantal to Franklin, who looked anxious to say the least. He beat his tail on the water, causing a splash to wash over the embankment where they stood.

The major didn't budge. "The whale likes you, doesn't he?"

Chantal nodded.

"I've seen that he obeys you," he said. "That he understands what you want him to do. Is that true?"

She shrugged.

The major cocked his head slightly, as if doubtful. "This is not the time to be modest."

Chantal nodded again, hoping her cooperation might soften whatever the major had in store for her, for Franklin, for Aunt Sophie.

"Good," the major said. His shadow fell across her. "Do whatever you must to keep him here. Make him feel safe and welcome."

Chantal's breath caught as though a hand were

squeezing her throat. What the major ordered was the very thing she didn't want to do. What she desperately wanted was to tell Franklin to swim away as fast as he could and never come back. To retreat and protect himself. To go where he'd be safe.

In her mind, Chantal spat on the ground very near the major's boots.

He pushed her toward the river's edge. "Do as I say, girl."

Chantal stared into Franklin's sad and trusting eyes. It would break her heart to lie to him. She glanced over at Aunt Sophie, who was lying in a heap, not moving at all. Chantal broke out in a sweat. A sick tingling traveled over her body. There was no way around it. German orders were absolute.

"Stay, Franklin." Her voice trembled. "You're safe here. There's nothing wrong."

Franklin had heard her words. Of this, she was certain. Whether or not he believed them was impossible to say.

He winked.

She winked back.

Such a sly whale, she thought. He stayed.

"News of the whale has reached the Führer," Major Wölfflin said, his voice strident and soaring into the sky. "The whale is a sign of good fortune. Not for you, but for us. Your heroes will never take Normandy. We are blasting them. We are making soup out of them!"

The major's report fetched a deep groan from the crowd. For once, the Germans weren't lying.

"The great storm," the major went on, "swallowed their fleet." He gave a loud chuckle. "They will never reach Paris."

Chantal stared at the people in the crowd. Like her, they seemed overwhelmed by misery. And fury. Fury at Major Wölfflin, and fury at this long, tiring war. Fury at the Germans, who were holding their land in thrall. Fury at those who sought to rule their fate to their dying day, and their children's fate, and their children's children's fate.

The major wasn't finished. "The Führer wants the whale to remain in Paris, and for no harm to come to him. He will be placed in the new aquarium we will build once the war is over."

A fierce dread descended on Chantal. An aquarium? The only thing worse than being trapped in the Seine was to be trapped inside a tank. She imagined Franklin within, shivering and restless, stuttering a single syllable again and again. Or he would endlessly howl and gnaw at the glass walls, his corrosive tongue sanding away at the surface, though never all the way through.

She heard the sound of snapping and popping, and

realized Major Wölfflin was crouching beside her. His heavy arm slung around her shoulders, as if they were a team, a united front. A vile smell escaped from his uniform: gamey sweat and something like wet dog. Chantal held her breath.

"If anyone other than the girl touches the whale, I will shoot that person myself."

The arm was so heavy that Chantal began to feel her knees buckle. How she wanted to shrug that arm off! The moment she couldn't take it any longer, the major released her.

"I am counting on you to protect him," he said to Chantal in an exaggerated voice, making sure those on the quay heard him. "A soldier will be assigned to help you guard the creature day and night. If you fail to protect the whale, your entire family will be killed. I will shoot them in front of your eyes. Is that clear?"

Chantal nodded once. Her head was the only thing she could move on her stunned body. Major Wölfflin and his entourage mounted the steps of the embankment. The silence they left behind was terrifying.

Once she regained the use of her limbs, she rushed to Aunt Sophie and helped her sit up. The gardeners and onlookers slunk away, casting venomous glances back at Chantal, as if she alone had sentenced them all to die of hunger.

23

PRISONER

Workmen lowered strong nets into the river: one at Pont de la Tournelle, another at Pont Saint-Louis, and a final one at Pont de l'Archevêché.

German orders.

While Chantal watched the orders being carried out, waves of anger rolled through her. Franklin was trapped in the narrow strand of the Seine in front of her apartment building. The sight was crushing. Her whale, a prisoner. He would never see his family again. If the Germans won the war, he'd be put into an aquarium, an even smaller jail.

When Papa joined her on the quay, she was reminded of how she had put him and Aunt Sophie in harm's way.

He tried to joke around the gravity of the situation. "The major was bluffing, *cherie*."

"No, Papa. He was very serious."

Papa hadn't been there yesterday when Aunt Sophie was knocked down by a rifle. He hadn't been there when Major Wölfflin had threatened them with murder. Papa needed to understand that their lives were in danger.

Or did he already know?

As chance would have it, Private Schröder was the German soldier assigned to help guard Franklin. He was the same private who'd stopped by Chantal's classroom only weeks ago. The same private whose teeth were too big for his mouth, a flaw he was still unable to mask with his wispy mustache.

"I don't need your help," Chantal told him when he reported for duty. Of course she *did* need his help, she couldn't stay awake around the clock, but she refused to admit it.

"These are my orders," said Private Schröder.

"Orders, orders," groaned Chantal. Couldn't these Germans think for themselves? She bit her lip in self-rebuke. Had she thought for herself, when her orders had been to tell Franklin to stay?

Chantal crouched near the river, and Franklin swam up to her so she could stroke his head. He hadn't sung or rolled all day. Not once. She wished she'd been brave enough to ride on his back when he'd been free and willing.

"You've put him in jail," she said.

"It's for his own safety."

His own safety? Words such as "safety" and "orders" had taken on twisted meanings during the war.

By the end of the day, Chantal was exhausted. Her hunger depleted her energy and made her drowsy long before bedtime. Sitting on the stone steps, she could hardly keep her eyes open.

"Mademoiselle," prodded Private Schröder, "why don't you go home and get some sleep?"

"Franklin needs me."

"I can take over from here. You can't watch him day and night."

"He doesn't know you."

"Well, you can introduce me."

Chantal's eyes popped open. She hadn't expected Private Schröder to show any interest in her marine friend. It was probably a trick. What lay behind it was impossible to know. Germans were schemers, deceivers.

"Meeting a whale," he said, gazing at the Seine,

"would be the only good thing to come out of this war."

Now Chantal was truly surprised. In her mind, the Germans had come to conquer, not to meet whales. She searched for a good reason to refuse Schröder's request. Finding none, she approached the water and called, "Franklin! Franklin!"

The whale surfaced and made several croaks in a row followed by a long *aaach*. Chantal patted his back.

"May I touch him?" Schröder asked.

Chantal wanted to say "no," yet she felt it wasn't up to her. "Ask Franklin."

Private Schröder placed his gun on safety and slung it around his shoulder. He dropped to one knee beside Chantal and said, "Hello, Mister Franklin. My name is Oskar Schröder. Is it okay if I touch you?"

Chantal was uncertain whether Franklin would comprehend, but he must have understood something, for he made his usual pattern of five evenly spaced clicks—a sign of agreement.

She was taken aback. "He said 'yes.'"

Private Schröder reached out, and Chantal showed him where he could touch Franklin's head, away from his eyes and blowholes. Schröder rubbed his hand over Franklin's bumpy skin, and for the first time, she saw the private smile.

"*Wunderbar*," he said. (Wonderful.) He slid his hand

back and forth over Franklin, who made a series of chir-rups that sounded like snickering.

"Don't tickle him," Chantal warned. "Keep the pressure consistent. And never, ever touch his blowholes. He breathes from there."

"He's not a fish?"

"No. Whales are mammals, just like us."

She regretted what she'd said almost immediately. There was no "us" on the embankment. There was a French girl and a German soldier and nothing more. But Schröder caught Chantal's eye and offered another smile, suggesting he appreciated being included in the same class of organisms.

Franklin eased away from Schröder's hand and drifted off.

"I'm not sure he trusts you," Chantal said.

The private nodded and studied the whale with what seemed like a sad recognition, as if he knew what it was to be a confined creature, trapped in a world of someone else's design.

"Trust takes time," he said.

Chantal allowed the private to guard Franklin alone that night.

For the first few hours, she kept a close eye on them from her bedroom window, six stories above. She watched

Private Schröder on patrol, marching up and down the embankment, his boots thumping against the stones. His body was so stiff and his movements so clocklike, he resembled a toy soldier that a child had overwound.

Franklin swam beside him from one net to another like a pacing sleepwalker. He seemed entirely confused by his new confinement.

If only Franklin had left Paris when he'd had the chance. If only she had encouraged him to swim downstream and rejoin the sea.

She should have. She could have. He would have found his way home.

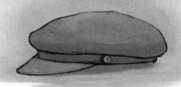

24

WHISPERS

The next morning, while Papa slept after a night of fishing, Chantal ate half an apple for breakfast, grabbed her ukulele, and returned to the Seine to be with Franklin.

"How was your night?" she said, rubbing the whale's cheek.

"Tdahhhh, ick, murhoooooma," he said, which meant either "Less worried than before" or "Better than yester-day." Had he felt safe with Private Schröder? Perhaps.

The German lay snoring.

On the Pont de la Tournelle, three men were watching Franklin. Hungry Parisians, looking like they were up to no good, obviously waiting for the moment when he would be left undefended. Some people might risk death by Major Wölfflin's firing squad rather than slow, torturing hunger.

Chantal nudged Private Schröder's boots. He climbed to his feet and stood at attention. Was he confused or making a joke? She was in no mood for joking. Her eyes flitted in the direction of the three men on the bridge.

"Oh, them." Schröder sighed. He aimed his rifle at the centermost man. All three of them scurried off.

Chantal was shocked by how quickly the joking private had turned dangerous.

"All you Germans are monsters," she heard herself say, immediately regretting the words. In times of war, it was dangerous to speak your mind.

The private's shoulders dropped, as did his gun. "I was only trying to scare them."

Schröder retired under the bridge to sleep some more. Chantal played a new song for Franklin on her ukulele, but he wasn't interested. All through the morning and into the afternoon, his eyelids drooped, as though he were constantly on the verge of sleep. How bored and frustrated he was!

Chantal was devastated. It was all so unbearably sad. She wanted to comfort him and cheer him up. But how? Franklin seemed to be in the midst of a whale-deep depression.

It was then that she came to understand just how much she cared for him.

Loving only a little was impossible. Once the heart opens up, there's no stopping it.

At the end of her shift, Chantal went to pay Odette a visit. Her feelings for Franklin had made her aware of how much she loved Odette and how little she'd seen her best friend lately. Odette's apartment was two streets over, closer to the Marais.

Chantal climbed the stairs and rang the doorbell. She rang it again and again. There was no answer. Finally the door opened. It was Odette's mother.

"What do *you* want?" she said.

"Is Odette home?" Chantal asked, wondering why Odette's mother was so annoyed.

"She's not here." Odette's mother shut the door, a censorious look on her face.

Chantal climbed down the stairs and crossed the street, then looked back. Was that Odette waving to her from the window? Or only a red drape unfurling in the breeze?

On the way home, people on the street averted their eyes from Chantal. There was whispering behind her back. It wasn't until a man called her a traitor under his breath that she realized that the Parisians associated her with the Germans. Major Wölfflin had defended her. He had swung his heavy arm around her shoulder. Franklin was the property of the Nazis. The darling of Hitler. In the eyes of Odette and her family, Chantal was a collaborator.

Shame came crashing down. Never before had her heart weighed so much in her young chest.

Curiously, the only person who didn't shun Chantal that day, who acted as if nothing had happened, was Father Maurice. His smile was warm and full of approval.

It made Chantal very suspicious.

That night, she lay awake in her bed and listened to a whispered conversation between Papa and Aunt Sophie coming from the other side of the sheet. She knew eavesdropping wasn't polite, but no one could blame her for the sheet not being soundproof. In a house without doors, there are no secrets.

"I'm telling you, Henri, they're not coming."

"Calm down. Of course the Allies are coming."

"No. The reports don't lie. They've decided to pass by Paris and march straight to Germany."

What? Chantal wished these words had passed *her*

by. A stone dropped into her stomach. If the Allies didn't come soon to liberate them, they would all starve.

Sophie said, "We're recruiting everyone. We need to retake the city ourselves. You must join us."

Chantal looked at the sheet, at the enlarged shadows of her father and aunt visible through the thin cotton. Was Aunt Sophie part of the secret rebellion, or what Papa called "the Resistance"?

Chantal had heard the rumors of small triumphs: road signs destroyed, the tires of German vehicles punctured, cut communication lines, bombed gasoline depots.

"You will bring them here," Papa said. "You will bring the Germans straight to our home. Then none of us will be safe."

"But I promised to fight."

Chantal drew in her breath and held it for as long as she could. A promise was forever.

25

A Wart or a Toothache

Chantal's world shrank. Besides Papa and Aunt Sophie, there was nobody who wanted anything to do with her anymore.

Except for Franklin, of course. And Private Schröder.

At first, Chantal kept their exchanges to a minimum, to prove that she wasn't a collaborator. But over time, Chantal and Schröder could be found having short conversations about Paris or Franklin or the small village where the private and his sister had grown up. The sister was Chantal's age, and the private missed her dearly.

Chantal began to see Schröder as less of a German soldier and more of a . . . well, she had difficulty completing that thought. It wasn't that Chantal was taking a liking to Private Schröder. It was more that she had grown accustomed to him, as one does to a wart or a toothache. What seems terrible at first can end up being tolerable.

From time to time, Major Wölfflin paid a visit to the quay. He inspected the nets and cross-examined Private Schröder. Had anyone approached the whale? Any suspicious activity? Schröder seemed as scared of the major as Chantal was. She had never seen him stand so tall and straight. Was his heart beating a mile a minute like hers?

One evening, when Private Schröder came to the Seine to relieve Chantal of her duty, he brought something unusual with him: a picnic basket.

Chantal was angry. How dare he eat in front of her, when he knew how hungry she was! When he was responsible for that hunger by being a German.

The private, however, didn't sit down to eat. Instead, he walked over to Chantal and offered her the picnic basket. "I brought this for you."

"For me?" She was hesitant to accept it. "Why?"

"To show you that I'm not a monster."

Chantal was proud that her bold words might have changed him. Was that the smell of bread rising from the basket? The hardened part of her heart melted a touch.

"Please," the private said, smiling. "Take it home to your family. Have a nice evening with them. I'll see you in the morning."

She accepted the basket and the risk.

Chantal raced up six flights of stairs, the picnic basket swinging in her hand. She dropped it on the kitchen table and opened the lid. Papa rushed over, still holding his newspaper. Sophie was fast behind him, craning for a look. There was a sausage from Lyon, two short loaves of bread, a stick of real butter, a pot of raspberry jam and a pot of goose liver pâté, ten potatoes (fist-sized), three apples plus two pears, and a small pouch of English tea.

Chantal's mouth began to water. What a feast they would have!

"*Incroyable!*" exclaimed Papa. (Unbelievable!)

Aunt Sophie said nothing.

Papa took three plates from the cabinet and a knife from the drawer. He kissed Chantal on the cheek. "Would mademoiselle care for a table by the window or near the *cuisine*?"

"Near the *cuisine*," said Chantal. "Close to the chef."

Papa gave her a broad smile and pulled out a chair. "Please, have a seat."

She did.

Aunt Sophie remained standing with her arms crossed as Papa sliced into the nutty-smelling bread. His hands moved fast yet with grace. He opened the pot of goose liver pâté and slathered some onto a piece. "Here, *cherie*. My own special recipe." Papa winked.

Chantal took the slice of bread from his hand and was about to open her mouth when Aunt Sophie spoke up.

"Where did this come from?"

Chantal didn't know whether to bite or respond.

"From the finest goose in all of France!" Papa said.

"Stop playing, Henri. Be serious."

His voice softened. "It doesn't matter where the food came from. What matters is that we eat it."

His reply seemed reasonable to Chantal, so she brought the piece of bread closer to her lips.

"Stop," commanded Sophie. "Answer me, Chantal."

Papa frowned and waved away Sophie. "Don't listen to her, *cherie*. Eat."

Chantal could smell how delicious the pâté would taste. If only her aunt would let her eat it.

"It's that German, isn't it?" asked Sophie. "The one who guards the whale."

"I don't care if the food came from Hitler himself," Papa said. "She's going to eat it!"

Chantal didn't know what to do. She desperately wanted to devour the pâté-topped slice, but the more her father and aunt fought, the more she hesitated.

"Henri Duprey," snapped Sophie, "that German must have given her the food as a reward."

"For what?" Papa said.

Sophie glared at Papa.

Suddenly Chantal understood. Sophie was worried that she had told Private Schröder about the radio.

"I didn't say a thing," Chantal said, her saliva almost overflowing. "Not about you or the radio."

The pâté smelled unbearably heady.

"Then it must be a bribe," Sophie said.

"Her stomach won't know the difference," Papa snapped.

Chantal couldn't resist any longer and crunched into the bread. The rich, scrumptious pâté melted fast, and the bread's yeasty zest flooded her mouth. Oh, the joy! How delicious it was. How *wunderbar*, as Private Schröder would say.

Of course the taste would have been even better if Aunt Sophie hadn't been shrieking: "You have to teach the girl some discipline!"

"Don't tell me how to raise my child!"

Although the two of them continued to fight, Chantal could barely hear them over the sound of the bread crunching. She closed her eyes and banished them from her mind. All that remained was the next bite and the crust scratching her gums and the goose liver pâté dissolving like creamy butter on her tongue.

26

DON'T LEAVE ME, PAPA

For the first time in a great while, Chantal awoke in the morning without hunger. The feeling was marvelous yet short-lived. When she slid back the sheet that divided the two rooms, there were no pillows on the floor where Aunt Sophie usually slept.

Last night, Sophie had been so angry at Chantal and Papa, she'd left the apartment with a theatrical slam of the door. It was almost funny at the time, but it wasn't funny now.

Had she stayed out all night?

Papa was still asleep on the daybed. Chantal got dressed quickly, stored the leftovers from the picnic basket in the kitchen cupboard, and went down to the river.

Even before calling Franklin, she handed the empty basket to Private Schröder and said, "Thank you."

The private smiled. "My pleasure."

"It was super-delicious," Chantal said, "but . . ."

"Yes?"

"Why are you being so nice to me?"

Schröder thought for a moment before answering. "If our situations were reversed and France had invaded Germany, I hope that a soldier like me would look after my sister."

Chantal was dazed, almost ready to believe him. What she felt stirring inside of her was warm and unguarded. It was nothing like the feeling you would have for a wart or a toothache. Scared of what the feeling might mean, she pushed it back down.

But during her day with Franklin, the very special whale now an island of sadness, she reflected on Schröder's conduct since the moment they'd met. He hadn't dragged her out of the classroom for questioning. Nor had he mistreated Franklin or been mean or rude. And then there was the gift of the picnic basket.

Shouldn't she judge him for his actions and not for his uniform?

Schröder returned that afternoon, alarmed. "I have bad news. Your aunt was arrested last night."

"Aunt Sophie?" Chantal jumped to her feet, fright seizing her. "Why?"

"She's in the Resistance."

Chantal froze. If he knew, then other Germans knew.

"Run to your father," Schröder said. "Tell him to leave. Soldiers are coming."

Was he telling the truth? Perhaps there was one way to know. "Who ratted me out about the submarine? Who told you?"

Schröder bit his lip and looked away as seconds passed. "Father Maurice. He's working for them . . . I mean us."

Chantal clenched her fist. "No, you were right to say *them*."

She arrived home to find Papa pacing. Worry was written all over his face. She knew exactly why.

"Your aunt still hasn't come back."

"The Germans took her," Chantal said.

Papa stopped pacing. "Yes, that's what I'm afraid of."

"Sophie's in trouble. We must go and help her."

"*I* will go and *you* will stay. But not here and not alone."

He opened the door and stamped down to the end of the hall. Chantal heard him knock, her heart thumping with each rap.

Papa returned with Professor Petit, who looked upset at having been disturbed. Chantal greeted him shyly.

Papa lifted her up and placed her on a kitchen chair. Standing like that, she was eye to eye with her father. He held her gently by the shoulders.

"Professor Petit will stay with you until I return."

There was an itch to protest—she didn't want to be treated like a child. But there was also a compulsion to obey. This was a time when you had to trust your father.

Papa went on: "After I leave, I want you to pack a small bag and go with Professor Petit to the church. Understood?"

"No."

"Please, *cherie*. Don't question. Do as I say."

Despite herself, Chantal started to cry. The apartment was no longer safe. *They* were no longer safe.

"Don't leave me, Papa. Please. Let's stay together."

Her father gave her a quick hug, then pulled back. His Adam's apple lifted and sank. "What about Sophie? I have to find her. I can't take you with me."

Chantal watched his mind and his feelings fight for dominion. Tears pooled in his eyes.

"I'll be back, *cherie*."

She nodded.

They embraced and Chantal buried her face in his neck. She inhaled his familiar smell, which seemed fainter somehow, although it was still comforting. Tobacco and leather and dark earth. Twice Papa tried to pull away and she wouldn't release him. Only when he said, "Please, *cherie*," did she let go.

There were no more words except for the essentials.

"*Je t'aime, Papa.*"

"I love you too, *cherie*." Papa kissed her on her forehead. "I'll see you soon."

He grabbed his coat and his hat and was out the door before Chantal could voice her darkest fear.

There's a storm coming.

27

A TERRIBLE ABSENCE

When Chantal and Professor Petit exited the apartment building, she turned left and he turned right. He stopped and ran after her.

"This way, Chantal," he said, cupping her elbow. "To Notre Dame and Father Maurice."

She shook off the professor's hand and continued in the direction of the stone steps that led down to the riverbank. It was already dark. She could hear Professor Petit shuffling behind her.

On the embankment, she found Schröder marching

back and forth. Professor Petit hurried to her side and shot the private an unfriendly look, recognizing him from the incident in the classroom.

Schröder extended his hand for the professor to shake. Petit did not shake it.

"It's okay," Chantal said to him. "You can trust Private Schröder." And then she added, as a good student might to a teacher: "People are not uniforms."

Did Chantal truly believe these words? The time had come to put them to the test.

Petit gave her a look of incomprehension. "Your father said to find Father Maurice."

"But he's one of them," she said. "A spy."

Petit's eyebrows sailed up. "What do you mean?"

"The submarine," said Chantal. "I told Father Maurice about it and he reported me to Private Schröder."

A whistle came from the professor's teeth. The sound was shrill enough to summon Franklin. The whale rose to the surface spewing jets of water and mist, making Petit startle back.

Chantal rushed toward Franklin. She crouched down and petted his head, and he purred with delight at seeing her. The water was as dark as the night. He screeched and made a series of snorts. Something was bothering him. Chantal looked up in the direction of the quay and her apartment.

One of the lights inside was on.

Chantal's heart leaped. "They're home!"

Another light turned on. In her bedroom, the window opened and a head popped out to look around.

The head didn't belong to Papa or Aunt Sophie. It belonged to a German soldier.

Chantal scooted into the shadows and felt herself grow very still. Professor Petit, who must have seen what she'd seen, was already there, standing beside the private.

"We must get you away from here," Schröder said.

"What about Papa?" she whispered. "Aunt Sophie?"

Schröder's eyes flitted as he made calculations. The air felt like it might crack. He took a hard look at Petit. "Monsieur, will you stay here with the mademoiselle until I return?"

With his one good arm, the professor loosened his necktie. "Where are you going?"

"To get answers," said Private Schröder.

Professor Petit looked at Chantal, then back at the private. "All right then, but be quick."

Chantal watched Schröder mount the stone steps leading up to the quay. She slipped out of the shadows to see her apartment building, and waited until he went inside.

"I don't know about this," fretted Professor Petit. His jaw was clenched.

"He's going to talk to the other soldiers and find out

what they know." Once again, Chantal wanted to believe in her words. Truth was, she couldn't be certain.

"What if he's telling them where you are?" asked Petit.

There were footsteps on the quay above them. They pressed themselves deeper into the shadows, keeping their backs against the stone wall.

"We should run," Professor Petit urged.

"Not yet," said Chantal.

A crashing noise came from her apartment building, the noise of a room being torn apart. The smashing continued for a long while and masked the sound of Private Schröder's descent down the stairs.

Unexpectedly, he was beside them in the shadows.

"After your aunt was captured last night," Schröder said, "she was brought to the commissariat. That is where your father went, to testify on her behalf. But they assumed he was also part of the Resistance and arrested him as well."

Chantal gasped. "No!"

Professor Petit placed his only hand on her shoulder to calm her. "Why are you telling us this?" he said to Private Schröder.

"Because . . . I want to help. When I was drafted, I said nothing. I could have died on the battlefield, but God spared me. I never knew why. Now I think he spared me so that I could help you."

"You'll get in trouble," Chantal said.

Schröder almost smiled. "Not if the Germans lose."

Chantal gave a quick nod. "If you want to help, take me to Papa and Aunt Sophie."

"It's too late."

Too late? A scream roared through Chantal's mind.

Private Schröder must have seen the terror on her face. "No, I mean to say, their stay at the commissariat will only be temporary. Within an hour, all prisoners will be on a train."

"Bound for where?" asked Professor Petit.

Schröder's jaw clenched. "A prison camp . . . the Frontstalag, in Rouen."

Somehow Chantal knew he was telling the truth. She could feel it—how Papa and Aunt Sophie would soon be gone. A terrible absence.

Anger rose high in her chest. Her mind raced with ideas, each of them hemmed in by fears and doubts. First Mama. Now Papa and Aunt Sophie. She couldn't stand to lose them. There was only one thing for her to do.

"I'll go to Rouen and find them."

"It's not safe," Petit said. "All of northern France is a battlefield. The roads have closed. The trains have stopped. There is no way for you to get there."

"No way," Chantal said, "except one."

The Long and Winding River

28

Narrow Escape

Chantal watched the Germans leave her apartment building. She returned to the sixth floor, bringing Professor Petit.

The rooms were in shambles, all of her and Papa's possessions flung into careless heaps. Drawers pulled out and overturned. Pillows slashed, their feathers floating everywhere. Contents of the armoire on the bed.

The radio was gone.

"Oh *mon Dieu!*" Professor Petit said. (My God!) "They will stop at nothing."

For a moment Chantal felt erased, as though she had disappeared along with Papa and Aunt Sophie. The Germans had kidnapped her family and trashed her life. What was left?

But there was something left, half-hidden in the mess from a drawer that had been overturned. Something that proved who she was: the photograph of her and Papa and Mama and Aunt Sophie. The photograph of all four of them together, smiling, arms thrown around one another.

Invigorated and reassured, Chantal stuffed the photograph into her pocket and got to work. She collected what she needed in a rucksack. She took Mama's ukulele and Papa's small fishing net hooped in metal. She took the waterproof wading overalls, once used by Aunt Sophie to surf-fish. She took the green rubber boots she wore in the garden and an extra pair of socks. She took a box of matches, a cork-top bottle filled with fresh water, and a small tin pan. She took the leftovers from Private Schröder's picnic.

When Chantal and Professor Petit made it back down to the quay, the private also had something prepared.

"What's this?" she asked. It was hard to see by the light of the moon.

"You'll need a harness," said Private Schröder. He had

buckled three or four rifle straps together, end to end, until they formed a sort of lasso.

Professor Petit took in what was happening with great disbelief. "No, this is not a solution."

Private Schröder shushed him.

Chantal called Franklin. He surfaced in a froth of bubbles and hissing water. She held up the harness. "Is it okay if I slip this around you?"

Franklin nodded.

She placed the harness in the water, and Franklin nudged his nose into it. The harness slipped past his jaws and fit snugly behind his eyes.

Franklin was ready for action, but Chantal began to doubt herself. Could she actually ride a whale?

She looked up at the abandoned apartment. She looked down at Franklin. Then she scouted the faces of Private Schröder and Professor Petit.

Her teacher was biting his nails, a sheen of sweat on his face. "I'm not at all sure about this—"

"I am," Chantal said. The words were meant to convince herself as much as him.

Professor Petit wouldn't let it go. "A whale is not a boat." He stamped his foot. "I meant it the first time: You *are* a silly girl."

"Quiet," urged Private Schröder. "She's better off on a whale than in a prison camp."

"Sometimes silliness is your best hope," Chantal said. She slipped on the waterproof overalls. They were too big, and Private Schröder had to roll up the cuffs several times. He winked at her.

The professor lowered his voice. "If you must go, then get out of the city and find some place to hide and wait."

"For what? For someone to rescue me? There isn't anybody left. My family is gone and the Allies aren't coming."

She jammed her foot into one of the green rubber boots. Thinking of the water's biting cold, she took her foot out and put on the extra pair of socks and tried again. A snug fit. She slipped on the other sock and the other boot.

"Is the coast clear?" she asked Private Schröder.

He looked up and scanned the quay. "For the moment, yes."

Chantal strapped the rucksack onto her back and secured the fishing net.

Then came the hardest part. Every child in Paris had taken a turn riding Franklin. Every child except her. Now there could be no more delay.

Franklin eased closer to the embankment like a water taxi waiting for a passenger.

Fear gripped Chantal as tight as a fist. She wanted to climb onto Franklin's back, but her feet remained cemented to the stone embankment.

Tears of frustration rose in her eyes. She stuffed them back down with thoughts of her mission. Papa and Aunt Sophie were on their way to imprisonment and possible death—she had to go and save them.

Chantal dug into the chest pocket of her overalls for the photograph. She looked at their faces: Mama, Papa, Aunt Sophie. Who would she be if she couldn't hold on to the people she loved?

She kissed the photograph and put it back into her pocket.

Franklin brayed a bit and let out a series of chirps. Was he encouraging her?

Chantal took a deep breath and placed one rubber-booted foot on his back. The whale stirred only slightly, his body tense and expectant. She placed her other rubber-booted foot on his back and knelt.

Don't look at the water, she told herself. Her eyes stayed on Franklin as she summoned her mother's courage and sat astride him. Her rubber-booted feet gripped his sides. It wasn't so scary. It was like riding a really fat horse.

Just as she was about to take off, Chantal remembered the nets attached to the bridges, blocking the Seine. She peered through the night in that direction.

Schröder followed her gaze, seeming to understand the predicament. From his belt, he unsheathed a knife.

He pondered something for a moment before relinquishing it to Professor Petit.

"A German gives me his knife?" her teacher said, looking perplexed.

Private Schröder waved away his bewilderment. "Go to Pont Saint-Louis and cut the net loose. After, you must run over the bridge and slash away the other side."

Professor Petit glanced at the knife in his hand.

Footsteps sounded on the quay. No, worse. Boots. *Schomp! Bluck! Schomp! Bluck!*

"Please, Professor," begged Chantal.

The boots rushed closer. Were they Major Wölfflin's?

"Hurry!" said Private Schröder. "It's now or never."

Finally, Professor Petit tightened his only fist around the hilt of the knife and rushed away.

Chantal clasped Franklin's harness.

"Thank you," she told the private.

He nodded. "I hope we will meet again, under better circumstances."

She smiled. "Me too."

"Halt!" came from behind them.

"You should go," he said, tapping Franklin on the head.

The whale was off in an instant.

Chantal's heart raced as Franklin sliced through the river. Water rushed over her knees, but she didn't feel it. She was waterproofed up to her chest. She held on for dear life, her hands clenching the harness. Franklin was so fast!

A gunshot fired behind her, then another. Bullets whistled past her head and pierced the water.

"Halt!"

Ahead of her, she could make out Professor Petit in the dark, hacking away at the end of the net attached to the bridge. She imagined his missing arm again, as strong as a gorilla's, helping his lonely arm succeed.

"Hurry, Professor!" said Chantal, even though he couldn't hear her.

Another bullet whizzed past.

Franklin was already approaching the bridge.

The net fell away from the right side and Professor Petit was on the run, across the bridge to the other side.

Franklin, however, was faster than the professor, and he was getting close, dangerously close. The professor wouldn't make it in time. If Franklin didn't turn around, he would be tangled in the net and their mission would be over.

What to do?

Chantal had led Franklin through a few uncomplicated maneuvers in the games they'd played, but could she manage the deft move she now needed him to make?

"Franklin, I want you to turn around and head in the opposite direction, and then turn back again."

He snorted in confusion and let out a loud bellow that echoed off the embankment. Chantal took this to mean: "No."

"Yes!" she insisted, yanking the leather harness to the left. A bullet zipped by on that side.

"Grooooolth!" said Franklin.

Professor Petit was still hacking away at the net.

"Turn!" Chantal said, pull, pull, pulling on the harness with more and more urgency.

At the last moment, Franklin veered left and avoided running into the net that Professor Petit hadn't yet managed to free from the bridge.

Now Chantal and Franklin were heading in the direction of the gunfire.

Bullets came faster. The reports of the rifles echoed all around.

Could she turn Franklin again? And if so, would Professor Petit be ready?

"Turn again," Chantal said, deciding to take the chance. "Do it!"

Franklin didn't seem to understand. Regardless, she kept tugging the harness toward the left. Finally, she felt him veer, though only slightly. Now they were headed for the riverbank.

"No!" Chantal shouted, and tugged again with every ounce of her strength.

Franklin started to swerve. Although it was a mild curve, it was wide enough to avoid hitting the bank. He kicked with his tail fin high in the air. Chantal felt herself slipping. Riding a whale wasn't easy.

Up ahead, the net was still in place on the left side of the bridge. She had faith, though, that the professor would make it.

Franklin balanced himself and made for the bridge. Time rushed forward with a vengeance. It was only a matter of seconds now.

"Hurry, Professor!"

More gunfire. More bullets. More hoarse-voiced shouts.

Franklin swam for all he was worth.

Professor Petit hacked with the knife, his one hand blurring with the effort. Up, down, back, and forth, until . . . the left edge of the net dropped into the Seine.

At that very moment, while Chantal held her breath and Professor Petit waved good-bye, the only whale Paris had ever known, and in all likelihood would ever know, sailed beneath the bridge and out to the world beyond.

29

WATER HORSE

Chantal hugged Franklin tightly. So tightly, she could feel his heart beating in a steady, calming way, throbbing up through his back and into her chest. An anchored *thud, thud, thud.* Her own heart, beating like a nervous bird's, began to slow and match Franklin's.

Although they were still going fast, Chantal relaxed a bit. Behind them in the distance, the gunshots ceased and the shouting faded to a murmur. The Eiffel Tower loomed to the left, dark and colossal. They were almost out of the city.

Whoosh, went Franklin's great fins. *Whoosh*. The sound was soothing and serene.

"Thank you, Franklin," she said, stroking his head. "You're doing great."

He purred in response.

Whoosh. The rocking motion of riding a whale was pleasant. River water sprayed gently over her knees, again and again. They were finally alone on the wide-open river. On the horizon, the moon was setting, the sky sinking into greater darkness.

Before long, Chantal was a puddle of exhaustion. With all the excitement dying down, she struggled to stay awake. It would be dangerous to fall asleep on Franklin's back. She could easily slip off and into the water without him noticing anything. He would keep swimming and leave her behind.

When they had traveled far enough for the night, she tugged on his harness and said, "Pull over." She tugged until he understood what she wanted and changed direction.

Chantal slid off his back onto the shore.

"I'm too tired to keep going," she said. "Please wait for me here, all right?"

Chantal retreated into the woods to use the bathroom, not that it was a real bathroom. For the first time, she saw the shared toilet in the hall of their apartment building as a luxury.

When she returned, Franklin was there, floating just off the shore.

She washed her hands in the river and drank a third of her bottle of water. She was hungry as well, but too tired to eat.

"Good night, my friend," she said as she fashioned a pillow out of her rucksack and found a soft, grassy spot to lie down. Before she knew it, her eyes were closed and she fell into a deep, well-deserved sleep.

The white nightmare did not come for her.

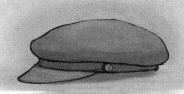

30

BATTLEFIELDS

Chantal awoke at sunrise, the sky red with energy. There was an instant when she didn't know where she was. Confused, she looked around. A burst of clarity came when she spotted Franklin in the river, floating with his nose in her direction as though waiting.

She was reminded of their narrow escape, their journey. Papa and Aunt Sophie. She balled her fists in resolve. No time to lose.

"Are you ready?" she asked.

In reply, Franklin flapped his tail, causing a wave to

wash over the shore. Birds scattered up, shrieking in protest. Chantal laughed.

Where would she be without him?

He swung over, but before she got on his back, she realized he was facing the wrong direction. "No. You have to swim *with* the current. *Downstream.* That's where the English Channel is." It took a burst of gesturing on her part to get the whale turned around.

Where would he be without her?

Although her stomach was already growling, demanding attention, she took no time for breakfast. She was eager to put more distance between them and Paris. After she drank some water, she climbed aboard Franklin, and together they set off anew.

What a fantastic thing it was, riding a whale! How snug and spellbinding, the smooth, constant motion. People had spent so much of history riding horses and donkeys and camels—who had thought to ride a whale?

But it made perfect sense: a pair of eyes above the water and a pair of eyes below. Together, Chantal and Franklin made a gigantic four-eyed creature with two brains and one mission: getting to Rouen.

She hadn't told him yet about her plans because she wasn't finished making them. She knew that Rouen was where Papa and Sophie were being held, and that the city was directly on the Seine, northwest of Paris. What the four-eyed, two-brained creature would do once it arrived in Rouen was unclear. Chantal didn't even know how long it would take them to get there. The Seine was hardly a straight line. It zigzagged and meandered in a chain of tight S's.

All this uncertainty didn't seem to bother Franklin. He just swam and swam and swam steadily down the center of the river, as though he understood their mission better than Chantal. Perhaps he enjoyed his release from prison so much, it didn't matter where they were headed or why. It only mattered that he was free.

Even though the sun was only two fingers over the hills, Chantal wasn't cold. Her wool socks and waterproof overalls kept her comfortable. But they didn't fill her stomach. She was getting hungrier and hungrier, yet Franklin was making such good progress, she didn't want to stop him. Breakfast would have to be taken on the road—or the river, so to speak.

With her left hand, she held on to the harness, while her right hand reached behind her and rummaged through her rucksack. Soon she had taken hold of the stubby end of a sausage leftover from Private Schröder's basket.

She brought it to her mouth and took a bite. Absolutely delicious.

Chew slowly, she reminded herself. *Make the sausage last forever.*

Just as she was about to take a second bite, Franklin veered left with a jerk. Chantal only caught a glimpse of the floating log he was trying to avoid before almost slipping off his back into the chilly water. In the process of fumbling with the harness, something else slipped: the sausage nub.

She watched it fall into the water with a *ploop.* No!

If she was going to survive, she'd have to be more careful.

All through the day, Chantal watched the sun's slow passage across the sky. Nothing noteworthy happened, until in the distance, people appeared on the right riverbank.

German soldiers?

She squinted to sharpen her vision. No uniforms. No rifles. No black helmets too dull to reflect the light. These people were not soldiers. They were civilians or refugees, which in wartime was probably the same. They walked in small clusters, on their way to a place where there was no fighting.

As she passed them, Chantal looked at their faces: shell-shocked and hopeless.

Some of them stopped to point at her. The sight of a girl riding a whale was unusual. A few even waved.

Perhaps they'd heard about Franklin and her on the BBC radio broadcast. The old bright feeling of being somebody special returned.

She found herself smiling and waving to the people. She wanted to help them but didn't have enough food to share, and her only mode of transport was built for one.

All she had to give was music. Should she take her ukulele from the rucksack and play them a song? She decided against it. What if the ukulele slipped from her hands, like the sausage had, and ended up at the bottom of the Seine?

Once Chantal and Franklin were alone again, the landscape changed from green bluffs to a bleak terrain. Blasted-out cars speckled the hillsides. There was the smell of charred wood in the air, with a chemical tinge that spoke of recent explosions. Her eyes began to sting.

They came upon the smoldering remains of a village. What destruction! On the left bank were abandoned houses of brick and wood, half-rising like broken skulls. Their beams were splintered, their roofs caved in or gone. Jagged glass was all that remained of the eyes that used to be windows.

This was what the refugees had fled. This was the

evidence of the war's destruction that she'd only heard about but not seen until now.

All along the river, debris was strewn about, littering everything. Did the rest of France look like this? The rest of Europe?

This was her country destroyed. The communities, the schools, the markets. Everything her ancestors had built, gone.

They floated past bricked streets torn asunder.

Hearths crushed.

Burnt toys left scattered.

And then: a body sprawled facedown on the riverbank.

Chantal squeezed her eyes shut against the horror.

"Don't look," she said. "Don't look."

Franklin didn't look. He didn't have to. He kept his eyes below the surface, in the kingdom of water where man couldn't go.

Perhaps it was better to be a whale, Chantal thought, to live under the sea, rather than witness the scoured and barren world.

On land, humans had made a mess of things. They talked about love and equality and peace, but in the end, war always won.

Yes, it was better to be a whale.

Whales didn't lie or betray one another. Whales didn't shoot one another or burn one another's homes.

Whales didn't put one another on trains bound for prison camps.

The sea was spared the foolishness of mankind.

Riding on Franklin's back past the smoldering remains of the village, Chantal thought her darkest thought: Maybe humans deserved to perish for what they'd done.

31

A RECIPE FOR BEETLES AND GRUBS

After passing the destroyed village, Chantal steered Franklin to the shore. The sun was just about to set.

She sat on a tree stump by the riverside and ate the final leftovers from Private Schröder's basket—the last slice of bread, smeared with the last of the butter and the last of the raspberry jam.

Each morsel was delicious while it lasted, yet afterward she was still hungry. What more could she eat?

Fishing would take too much time. She had to sleep, and the next day, they had to keep moving.

Could she trap and kill a rabbit? Unlikely.

There were plants and mushrooms growing all around her in the woods, but she had no idea which ones were poisonous. She was only familiar with the herbs and flowers and vegetables that grew behind Notre Dame.

The thought of the murderous gardeners made her shiver. Their desperate faces, their savage intentions. And Father Maurice. His warm eyes and cassock had convinced her to trust him. Convinced her wrongly. People are not uniforms—something she would never forget.

Chantal studied the earth beneath her feet. She kicked a large stone, flipping it over. No insects. Surely if she overturned enough stones, she'd find earthworms underneath. Beetles and grubs in the bushes. They were edible, right? Her stomach twisted in complaint.

Desperate, she settled on a bunch of dandelions, remembering how Papa had once added them to a salad. At the time, the flowers had been tasty and exotic. Now, in the dark, they were bitter and sandy in her mouth.

Curled up on her nonexistent bed, Chantal thought again about the earthworms and beetles and grubs. Her body wouldn't notice the difference between eating a handful of insects or a ham sandwich. But how awful they would taste! Papa would know how to prepare an earthworm. He would have the best recipe for beetles and grubs.

Would mademoiselle care for a table by the forest or near the river?

The river, please.

Our specials tonight are leaf crêpes with earwigs, aphid mousse, and grilled blue-winged grasshoppers.

Hmmmm. Sounds delicious. I'll have them all.

Chantal drifted off to sleep, hungry and alone. In her dreams, she chewed a wad of moths. Their dusty wings and furry abdomens blotted her mouth dry.

FISHING WITH FRANKLIN

The following day, the sun came back and brought the Earth with it. All the shades of green and brown surrounded her, and the sky was a convincing blue. She waded into the water and climbed onto Franklin's back. Together they headed down the river.

Whoosh, went Franklin's great fins. *Whoosh*.

But the day grew long. Riding a whale was marvelous for an hour or so. After that it became hard, wet work. Her hands were cramped and blistered from constantly clenching the harness.

To keep her spirits high, she talked to herself.

She was a girl on a whale, a girl on a mission.

She was a victorious warrior on her way to battle the enemy.

She was the brave daughter Papa and Mama would have wanted her to be.

But who was she kidding?

She was a lonely fugitive, a poor thing on the run.

She was a small, insignificant creature on the back of a whale.

She was a tired and hungry girl, longing for a warm meal, something to drink, and a dry bed.

Chantal couldn't deny that she longed for Papa and Aunt Sophie, and most of all, for Mama.

Would it ever get easier? Would she ever stop missing what was missing from her life?

She bent down to hug Franklin, her one true friend. Perhaps he, too, longed for his mother. Perhaps, like her, he lived part of his life in the past.

By late afternoon, Chantal's stomach cramped up in emptiness. She desperately needed to eat. If only she could be like Franklin, who ate as he swam. He didn't need to stop in order to fish. There was something to be learned here.

Chantal paid attention. All Franklin had to do was

swim with his jaws slightly open and wait for the fish to be trapped inside. After a while he'd close his mouth and force the water out of his baleen. This made a fizzy sound. Whatever remained in his mouth, he swallowed.

She began to notice certain signs when Franklin "fished." Somehow he knew in advance when it was time to open his jaws, as though he could sense that there were schools of fish ahead. Franklin was a very smart whale.

Chantal took advantage of his intelligence. As soon as she felt Franklin open his jaws, she slipped Papa's net into the water, just beside Franklin's head. And . . . bingo! She caught the first fish of her journey, a small trout, and soon after, two golden-gray mullets.

Tonight, she would have a feast.

When the last orange rays of sunlight were wrung from the sky and darkness reclaimed the hills, Chantal halted Franklin.

On shore, she collected birch bark, moss, pinecones, and sticks, and assembled them into a small pile. From her rucksack she removed the box of matches and struck one, setting the flame into the tinder.

The day had been dry, and soon the wood snapped and crackled.

She filled her tin pan with river water and boiled the

water to kill the germs. No, she wouldn't die of thirst, not with the mighty Seine at her feet.

It was time to try her hand at roasting the fish. She staked them on sticks and held them above the flames.

Franklin watched her from where he floated in the Seine. Curiosity shone from his eyes. Being a whale, he'd never seen one of his meals roasted over an open fire.

The trout was fatty and cooked slower than the two mullets. When they were done, Chantal took her first bite, plucking the flesh directly off the bones. Although there was no salt with which to season the fish, the taste was splendid all the same.

Papa would have been proud.

Franklin seemed motivated to swim farther and farther each day, never growing tired. Chantal felt grateful for his determination, for how he adopted her mission as his own.

Or had he?

As they advanced, Chantal realized there was probably something else that was keeping Franklin motivated: He was keen on going home. But his home was farther than where she needed to go. Farther than Rouen.

If she stayed behind, could he complete the journey

by himself? In the mornings, he often faced the wrong direction. Obviously, this shortcoming of his was why he'd ended up in Paris.

What would happen if she weren't there to direct him? Would he find his way home?

33

LEBANON, KANSAS

One morning, five or six days into their journey, Chantal awoke to a new feeling. Something told her to be extremely vigilant from this point on. At any moment, she and Franklin would reach Rouen, the city where the enemy waited.

"Okay, Franklin," Chantal said, climbing on top of him. "Be on the lookout for the Germans. They might be in boats. They might be in bunkers along the river. If they're hiding in the trees, I'll spot them and warn you."

Although it wasn't much of a pep talk, it was all she could manage.

Off they went. Fog gobbled up the river as the morning progressed.

Chantal felt her senses sharpening. Every so often she stopped breathing to listen. Still, she only heard the swish of Franklin's fins and beyond that, the lapping of the waves against the shore.

By the middle of the day, a beam of sun broke through the fog. It sparked off the tall, single spire of Rouen's Cathedral. The ramparts were ghostly in the distance.

Triumph washed over her. They'd made it!

"Easy does it, Franklin. Not too much splashing."

His fins stroked the water with a greater deliberation as Franklin swam as stealthily as he could.

Chantal saw the first of the destroyed bridges. She steered Franklin around the piles of broken masonry and kept him to the far left, where a small woods faced the city's stone walls.

The fog was thickest along the riverbank. Was it enough to hide them?

Chantal shuddered, recalling the white nightmare, the tendrils reaching out to grab her ankles. But given the choice between fog and bullets, she preferred fog. She tucked Franklin into the mist, hoping it would make them invisible.

"We have to wait for nightfall," she said. "Then we can save Papa and Aunt Sophie."

He let out a small chirrup of excitement.

How would they save them, though?

"What do you think is the best plan of attack?" Chantal asked.

With a purr, a cluck, and several squeaks, Franklin contributed his ideas to the discussion. She shook her head. "We can't swim up to them. The camp is probably not on the river."

He piped and barked.

She shook her head again. "No. I don't think there are any canals that travel from the Seine into the city."

He growled with frustration. They would have to think of something better.

Chantal pulled Franklin over to the riverbank and parked him. She climbed off his back and waded to the shore, careful not to dunk her rucksack and drown her ukulele.

"Stay low," she told him. "I'll be right back."

In the woods, the fog had already lifted. Emerald light shone through the canopy of lush leaves, dazzling greenly.

She headed into the trees. Broken spider webs clung to her cheeks. From somewhere, she heard a hidden stream.

The desire for clear, sparkling water overwhelmed her. Chantal found the stream. She crouched and scooped up some water and drank. Cool and delicious. She scooped and drank again and again.

There was a sound then, off to the left, a rustle in the scrub like pine needles crinkling underfoot. Chantal froze.

"Hello, there," a voice said in English. A man's voice.

She wheeled around in combat stance. All she saw, however, was forest and trees. Where had the voice come from?

The rustle in the scrub came again, this time from the right. Chantal refocused her gaze. The air was still, yet all around was the impression of movement—subtle, secret, shifting.

From one of the bushes a figure emerged, and Chantal startled back. At first it seemed like a man made of forest or a tree that could walk. The tree removed its head. Chantal saw the dirty face of a man.

"It's okay," he said, smiling. "Don't be afraid. I won't hurt you."

He spoke English with a funny accent. It didn't sound like what she'd heard on the BBC or in her English class. Where was he from? She studied him with greater attention. The head he'd removed was actually a green helmet wrapped in twigs and leaves—not a German helmet.

Then she caught sight of a small flag stitched onto the sleeve of his uniform. Stripes of red and white and stars on a field of blue.

Her heart jumped. "You're American!"

"That I am, indeed."

Chantal unclenched her fists and smiled for the first time in days. From behind the man, more forest-green soldiers emerged from the vegetation. They'd been watching her all along, and she never knew it.

The man was thin, his body wired with energy. He extended his hand for Chantal to shake. "Colonel Roger Myles, US Army, Fox Company, at your service, young lady."

She shook his hand. "I am very pleased to meet you."

"You speak English pretty well," said the colonel.

She nodded and released the colonel's hand. Everything was becoming less worrisome and more interesting.

The colonel brushed back a tree branch and pointed across the river to where the city sat, its stony ramparts patrolled by German soldiers. "Is that where you're from? Rou-en?"

Chantal giggled at his pronunciation. He had turned the city into two, incomprehensible words. "Rouen," she said. "It's one sound, one word."

The men behind the colonel chuckled and drew closer. Colonel Myles crouched down and balanced his helmet on his knee. "I suppose my French is pretty rusty. I'm from Lebanon, Kansas, which happens to be the geographic center of the United States . . . about as far from Europe as anyone can get."

From inside his vest pocket he produced something small and rectangular, wrapped in dark paper and foil. He tore open the package and handed it to Chantal.

Her mouth watered.

How many years had it been since she'd tasted chocolate?

"Go on," the colonel said. "You look hungry."

Chantal studied the colonel's face uncertainly. A satiny scar laced through an eyebrow.

"We can split it," she suggested, not really wanting to, yet trying to be polite.

"Don't worry," the colonel said. "There's plenty more where that came from."

His voice was calming. There was a kind of music in it, a sad music.

Chantal took the chocolate from the colonel and bit into it. The sweet, velvety succulence spread over her tongue, and for a brief moment she was in a state of bliss. Other than Papa's salmon quiche, or more recently Private Schröder's goose liver pâté, the chocolate was the best thing she'd ever tasted.

Her eyelids closed and fluttered. When she opened

them, she looked over the colonel's shoulder at the men who were still coming out of the bushes and the trees. She counted thirty, maybe forty men, their faces and hair streaked with mud. Sunlight filtered through the green leaves attached to their helmets.

Chantal blinked. "You got trapped in the *bocage*."

The colonel stood and brushed his hand across his forehead. "That we did. We lost too many good men and our amphibious vehicles."

Chantal had no idea what amphibious vehicles were and, not wanting to show her ignorance, refused to ask for a clarification. "But now you're here, to save us." She was taking smaller bites of the chocolate, hoping to make it last.

"Yes, we are." A glint of pride in his eyes.

"So let's go."

"Go where?" he asked, seeming reluctant to move from the cover of the woods.

"First, you have to save my father and my aunt. They're in a prison camp that way." Chantal pointed to the town across the river. "And then you have to free Paris."

Colonel Myles grinned. "I'd like nothing better than to free everyone." He swept another branch aside. "But first we have to cross that river. You see, the British bombed the bridges over the Seine—"

He pronounced it as though it rhymed with "lane."

"It's the Seine," she interrupted, making it rhyme with "hen."

The soldiers laughed again. Chantal was on her last bite of chocolate.

Colonel Myles continued, correcting himself. "The Seine. The British bombed the Seine so the Nazis couldn't get any tanks and trucks across it to attack us. Now we've got Normandy pretty well sewn up."

"What does that mean?" Chantal said.

"That means we got it. We won it."

Her heart leaped high in her chest.

"But this river is where our victory ends," Colonel Myles went on. "If we can't cross it, we can't capture the town."

Chantal scanned the group of men. Could they do it alone?

The colonel smirked as if reading her mind. "Don't underestimate us. Forty good men can take a town, but not with our guns wet."

Her stomach churned with the chocolate and the potential bad news. But it didn't have to be bad news, not if a solution was at hand.

"If I can get you across the river," she said, "will you promise to save my father and my aunt?"

Colonel Myles turned serious. "If you can get us across that river, I'll do anything you ask."

34

HOLY COW!

Chantal led the colonel and his men down the path she had taken through the woods. As soon as the tree cover began to thin, the men fanned out. Some crouched, some crawled on their bellies and lifted binoculars to their eyes.

Colonel Myles stayed behind with his men while Chantal returned to the riverbank. She expected Franklin to be right there where she'd left him, which wasn't the case. Where did he go? Her eyes swept the river. The mist had cleared. The whale was nowhere in sight.

A flash of panic. Was he captured? Did he swim away? Or had Franklin taken her advice to "stay low" too literally—was he waiting underwater?

Chantal unshouldered her rucksack and removed her mother's ukulele. The mother-of-pearl inlay glinted in the sunlight. She strummed the first two chords of her and Franklin's song, "Somewhere Over the Rainbow."

The whale didn't surface.

Apologetically, she glanced back at Colonel Myles, who'd crept closer. Only his face and shoulders could be seen from within the tangle of bushes. He was giving her an uneasy smile.

"Let me try again," Chantal said.

She played the chords once more.

And she waited, again in vain.

Panic coursed through her. Where was Franklin? He usually surfaced with those two magical chords.

"Franklin!" she called, cupping her hands into a megaphone. "Franklin!"

"Who is Franklin?" Colonel Myles asked.

"My friend. He's a whale."

At this, the colonel's men laughed like it was the most hysterical thing they'd ever heard.

The colonel, however, was not laughing. He wore the face of a weary, disappointed man. A man tired of waging war in the rain and the muck. A man facing a wide, racing river, with no way to cross it. A man lied to by a silly girl.

He signaled to his men. The soldiers climbed to their feet and started shuffling away.

"Where are you going?" Chantal asked.

Colonel Myles stopped. "Darlin', we've got to get a move on. There's a Nazi battalion behind us. We can't stay."

"You have to."

"No, we really can't." A slight edge to his voice.

Chantal felt betrayed. Had Franklin deserted her? She remembered how motivated he'd been to come this far, and how she'd wanted to pretend that he'd done it all for her. Of course he hadn't. He was just as eager to find his family as she was to find hers.

Franklin must have sensed that she intended to go with the soldiers to find Papa and Aunt Sophie. He somehow knew that she might abandon him. What a lousy friend she was. She had been selfish, only considering her needs, her losses, her broken heart.

She stepped back to the shore. "I'm sorry, Franklin."

Next she shouted it: "I'm sorry, Franklin! I won't leave you behind."

She paced up and down the shoreline, knowing that her next words needed to be chosen carefully. Franklin was no fool. He expected more from her, something of great importance to demonstrate her sincerity. Something that, once said, can never be reversed.

"I promise!"

Two magic words held in high esteem in her family. Audacious words. Just saying them made it difficult for Chantal to breathe. It made her vulnerable to the forces of the future, to what lay ahead, good or bad.

Chantal stopped pacing. "I promise. You brought me to my family, and now I'll bring you to yours. I promise!"

The words took effect almost immediately. Gigantic bubbles broke the surface of the water. The woods themselves began to shake. Colonel Myles and his men must have halted and turned around, for she felt them rush up behind her. They were just in time to see a whale emerge from under the green, flowing river, causing Colonel Myles to exclaim: "Holy cow!"

They waited for nightfall. As soon as the clouds covered the moon, Franklin ferried his first soldier across.

Upon the whale's return, Colonel Myles shook his head. "This is going to take too long."

Chantal climbed down to the water's edge. "Franklin, can you take two men across at a time?"

Franklin made a *cluck*, a *dook*, and a long *neigh*.

"I think," said Chantal to the colonel, "he can take two men and a little bit more."

Chantal was right. Franklin must have been feeling strong and energetic, because he was able to take two men at a time across the Seine. Two men and their weapons.

By one in the morning, he'd transported the entire company. The last passengers were Chantal and Colonel Myles.

The colonel grabbed on to the harness and stepped aboard Franklin. Chantal could tell that he didn't want to smile, that he didn't want to make light of such a serious event. Still, nothing could keep him from saying, "In the nonsense of war, everything makes sense."

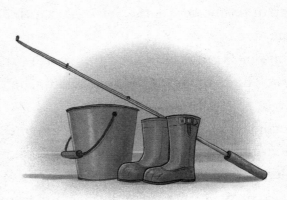

35

A PROMISE

On the other side of the river, Chantal borrowed a piece of paper and a pencil from one of the American soldiers. After she was finished writing, she folded the letter into thirds and gave it to Colonel Myles.

On the outside flap was printed: FOR HENRI DUPREY.

In the colonel's hand, the paper crackled and sighed.

"I made a promise," she said.

His lips tightened into a grim line. Chantal let the silence tug between them.

Franklin floated in the river, waiting.

It was hard to leave Papa and Aunt Sophie behind—no, it was more than hard. Almost impossible. She wanted to rush to them, hold them in her arms, reunite with them right here and now.

But the truth was, they had Colonel Myles and forty American soldiers to save them, and Franklin had only her. She couldn't send him off on his own, not after all he had done. She would have to leave her family behind to find his. It was that simple.

She'd already mentioned this to Colonel Myles and didn't feel like explaining anything further. No matter what she said or did, he wouldn't approve of her going off alone with no one to depend on except a whale. The colonel wouldn't understand that Franklin was the smartest, most dependable whale she'd ever met. Well . . . the only whale she'd ever met.

She preferred to think that the colonel saw her as he saw himself: a soldier answering the call of duty. Professor Petit once explained that during times of war, soldiers often performed acts of valor and self-sacrifice that made little sense, yet had to be done.

She did not mention these things.

Nor did Chantal want to say good-bye, for she had come to like and admire the colonel, and it would only hurt her to admit that she'd probably never see him again.

All she did was salute him smartly, and he returned it without saying a word.

She trusted him to save the two people she loved most in the world.

36

CHANTAL'S LETTER

Dear Papa and Aunt Sophie,

I'm sorry I'm not there. I'm with Franklin on my way to the sea.

When he arrived in Paris, he was all alone. Far from home. He was a friend to us, but we did not treat him like a friend in return.

Being at war was no excuse.

Franklin didn't hold a grudge. Not even against me. He saved my life. He brought me to Rouen and the

American soldiers to you. So I made a promise to help him find his family.

It breaks my heart not to be with you, but I made a promise.

I hope this letter reaches you and you're well enough to read it. If my mission succeeds, I will be in Honfleur, waiting for you. If not . . . please know that I tried my best, and I will live in your hearts as you do in mine.

Love,

Chantal

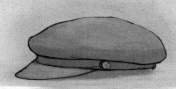

37

THE DARK FOREST

Whoosh, went Franklin's great fins. *Whoosh.*

They were on their own again, just Chantal and her whale heading for places unknown. Never before had she ridden Franklin all through the night. Regardless, her plan was to keep him swimming until dawn. Or until he gave out.

Walls of spiny trees loomed up on either side of the river. Everywhere was the scent of damp earth and mold spores. They were entering the dark forest.

She had seen it on the colonel's map, that somber

jade parcel sprawling between Rouen and the English Channel. She and Franklin would have to pass through the forest if Franklin was ever to make it home. There was no other way.

Soon the air chilled and the sky closed overhead. Large, frightful elms pressed inward. Their branches snaked every which way and trembled with wind.

Chantal wanted to be fearless, face the world head-on in rash confidence like Mama, but as Franklin swam, she grew more unsure about what she'd done, about leaving Papa and Aunt Sophie behind. About what lay ahead . . .

"Don't be scared, Franklin," she said in a small voice.

He let out a chirp.

In the light of the silvery moon, the forest was spooky. The winding of the river brought them to one primeval scene after another. Everything looked to be timeless, as if teeming with life from every era.

There were bats flitting on a hunt. Snakes slithering. Up in the trees feathery shapes perched on the branches. The black shapes of ravens. Under their watchful eyes, Chantal held on tightly to Franklin's harness.

The deeper they went into the dark forest, the more her eyes darted. She half-expected to come upon a cruel band of thieves or German deserters, but around each bend of the river, there were only more trees and more darkness.

Had she made a mistake by coming here?

From her pocket, Chantal removed the photograph of her and Papa with Mama and Aunt Sophie. All four of them together, a happy family. If Mama were still alive, she'd convince Papa and Aunt Sophie that Chantal had made the right decision. She'd be proud that her daughter was growing up and had honored her promise.

Leaving Rouen had been the right thing to do. Franklin deserved to be reunited with his family, to taste again the freedom of the open ocean. To be home.

They traveled through the night and deeper into the dark forest, the two-brained, four-eyed creature.

38

FIREBALL

An insistent droning began low and started to rise.

"*Shhhhh,*" Chantal said.

Franklin let out two bleats and a disagreeable bellow as if to say, *That's not me.*

If it wasn't Franklin making the sound, then what? Then who?

The droning grew louder and louder until it sounded like they were approaching a hive of giant bees, underscored by a low-pitched sound. A throbbing thunder that no insect, no matter how many of them, could produce.

Chantal gripped the harness tightly.

Franklin swam slower, his body tensing beneath her.

With the droning came a slight tremor, as if the ground beneath the river was quaking. This was followed by small cracklings in the air like static electricity.

"Groooothelsme," said Franklin.

"I don't know what it is," replied Chantal. As the words left her lips, her sense of foreboding deepened. She tightened the straps of her rucksack in preparation for what might be coming.

The droning was deafening and the moonlight was suddenly canceled out, as if by gigantic birds passing overhead.

Not birds, she thought. *Airplanes.*

The first bomb exploded seconds later, destroying a group of trees on the left bank. Fire and sparks leaped into the air. Chantal felt the shockwave travel from Franklin's body to the top of her head. He raged with a loud cry and banked right, away from the massive concussion.

Then came a great, flowing change of color. The dark greens of the forest gave way to oranges and reds, spreading in fireballs. Bombs whistled as they rained down. Now and again, flashes of bright white burst, like the bulb of a huge camera, followed by waves of rolling carmine sweeping through the tree trunks, tinting the entire forest.

"Swim, Franklin!"

The whale picked up speed, lurching with each *BOOM!* and *FRACK!*

More bombs exploded, sending split timber and wooden shards into the river. Chantal ducked and yanked Franklin's harness left and right, coaxing him out of harm's way as much as she could. The fire and debris were coming from every direction.

Who was flying these planes?

Gazing up, Chantal had her answer. There were black crosses outlined in white, emblazoned on the underside of broad wings. Germans. German planes.

Why were they attacking the forest?

The next explosion shocked everything white. The strobe, like a bolt of lightning, gave her a glimpse of soldiers, a whole battalion of them, fleeing through the trees. American and British soldiers.

The Germans were attacking the Allies, who were deep into enemy territory. She and Franklin were just in the way.

She peered over her shoulder. Behind them, the forest was completely ablaze. There was nowhere to go except forward.

Another blast of searing air poured over her. Chantal shut her eyes. Tiny daggers stabbed her face and neck. It was like being covered in hornets. She desperately wanted to rub the burning away, but Franklin was swerving and bobbing too much for her to let go of the harness.

His skin must have been burning too, for he blew a cooling jet of water out of his blowholes. Chantal welcomed the water splashing over her face.

The next bomb dropped even closer to them. Fire filled the sky and reflected red off the surface of the river. Streams of sizzling air snaked past her head.

Her hair was on fire.

Chantal screamed. Franklin yelped in pain. Both of them were burning. The smell was awful, the scent of hair singeing to her scalp.

Franklin dove and suddenly Chantal was underwater, the pain washing away.

She held her breath.

Please, Franklin, don't stay down too long. Not too long.

Her impulse was to release the harness, but then she'd lose Franklin, possibly forever. So she held her breath for as long as she could.

Then Franklin was up again and Chantal was gasping for air. Short, fire-filled breaths. The air blazed into her nostrils and throat. Air she didn't want, yet desperately needed.

Her throat scorching, Chantal coughed and retched.

Staying on the whale was nearly impossible. Franklin's

back was nothing but a slick, bucking dome. Up and down she went, commanding her hands not to let go, her body not to be caught off balance.

"Take it easy, Franklin!"

The whale appeared to have forgotten her. She was flung like a soaked rag doll, sloshing in and out of the angry waves. Without warning, she'd be up to her chin in river, or deep below, and then out of it, coughing and gasping for air.

Wave after wave, fireball after fireball, all unleashed in their direction.

There was nothing but bombs and Franklin.

The red sky above the planes was a mere blur. One of the aircraft erupted into flames. This was trailed by a series of sharp, screaming whistles to the right and then another huge explosion.

A tall tree splintered and began crashing down toward them.

"Left, Franklin, left!"

Franklin remembered his passenger and veered. Still, the tree fell too fast to be avoided. In a split-second, it would be crashing straight down on Chantal. She released the harness and slid down Franklin's back till she was astride his powerful tail fin. It was a disastrous mistake. With one mighty flick, he launched her into the air and over the falling tree, its branches swirling beneath her with flames. She landed in the river, the bubbling cauldron rising to meet her with a thunderous smack.

At least that's how it seemed before the red forest went black, darker than it had ever been.

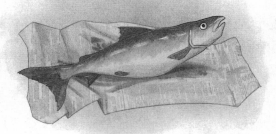

39

BLINKS OF BLUE LIGHT

Chantal plunged down. All at once the sound muffled, and the water was cold, so cold it strangled her breath. How could the water be so cold when the forest above was on fire?

Her teeth chattered. Shivers wracked her body. She kept sinking, looking around wildly in the darkness. Never before had she been so cold, so lonely.

She called out, but the words were only bubbles that floated away. She thrashed and made motions of swimming. Still, she sank.

So this was what it meant to be drowning.

Ever since Mama had died, Chantal had feared drowning. Surprisingly, that fear now started to fade. It was being devoured by the horrifying experience itself. An experience that drifted from alarming to dreamy and slow.

Blinks of blue light fluttered at her feet. The blue dots spread, dimming and flaring in a ring surrounding her like a phosphorescent storm.

Was this death coming for her? If so, it was more peaceful than she'd imagined.

Instinct told Chantal to swim away from the blue specks. Her heart, however, wanted to investigate them further. How alluringly they sparkled, these beautiful lights. As though they wanted to tell her something.

Chantal heard singing. At first she thought it was Franklin, but she soon recognized Mama's voice, the voice that always called to her from the water.

The blue lights swirled around her. A cluster formed a woman's face with kind features.

Mama?

The face of lights smiled and nodded. It was her! Exhilaration chased the cold from Chantal's body. Love warmed her bones, beamed through her muscles, and raced through her veins.

She had found Mama as she always knew she would, waiting for her beneath the harshness of the world.

Mama, I'm not scared! The thought leaped from Chantal's mind and sounded like words shouted over a canyon.

Mama smiled as though she understood. It was a soft, knowing smile that spoke of many things. The remaining blue specks gathered below her face and formed the shape of a woman, transparent and ghostly, and yet so real. She was Mama, without a doubt, wearing her finest silk dress.

They floated together until they came to rest on a rocky ledge.

"I've missed you so much," Chantal said.

"I've missed you too, *cherie*."

"Now we never have to be apart."

Mama smiled but shook her head. "*Cherie*, you can't stay with me."

"Why not?"

Mama gestured with a hand all around them. "This place is not for the living."

"But Franklin lives here, and he's alive."

"You're a girl, not a whale. A girl with an entire life ahead of you."

"I don't want to leave."

Mama made the face she used to make whenever Chantal said immature things. "Part of growing up is not giving up."

Although Chantal knew her mother was right, she reached out and tried to grab hold of Mama's hand. It slipped through her fingers like the slick fin of a fish.

"Time to go, *cherie*."

Chantal was unsure whether she could.

"You can," Mama said, reading her mind. "And you must. Dying is easy. It's those left behind who suffer the most."

Chantal had never thought of it that way.

At once she imagined Papa and Aunt Sophie receiving the news of her death, and how devastated they would be. She recalled how shattered they'd all been by Mama's death, a heartbreak they had to live with day after day and deep into every night.

For the living, the pain goes on forever.

4⦿

A WARM, SANDY PILLOW

Mama and the blue lights vanished and were replaced by pure darkness. Sound, too, was vacuumed away until only a muted, unexpressed world remained. Had Chantal gone deaf and blind?

She could feel the water draining out of the river, as though someone had pulled the plug from a giant bathtub. Impossible. Still, the water level dropped and dropped until Chantal's head surfaced above it.

She gasped for breath.

And another breath.

How strange it was to breathe air rather than water! But she was blind.

As the water continued to drain, Chantal explored with her hands. Beneath her was something that felt like a warm, sandy pillow. The roof was only inches above her head. Just in front of her were thin bars in a vertical row.

Where was she?

It was dark, as dark as the darkest room she'd ever been in. Cramped and wet and nearly silent.

And the smell was awful—so saturated and heavy, it seemed less of a smell than a pressure.

She returned her attention to the thin bars. *This must be the way out,* she thought, running her fingers along the bars from left to right. She heard a dull, tickling laughter. A laughter she recognized.

"Franklin!"

At once she understood that she was in his mouth. The warm, sandy pillow on which she sat was his tongue.

Franklin must have scooped her up from the bottom of the Seine, the way he would a fish.

Saved like Jonah.

"Franklin, let me out."

His jaws opened. Light and sound returned: the sizzle and snap of burning trees, distant explosions.

Chantal climbed out of the whale's mouth and

lumbered onto the shore, dizzy with lack of oxygen. Every muscle and bone in her body ached.

"That was a close call," she said, lifting her hand to her head, to where her hair had been. Much of its length had burned off. She ran her fingers over her face and felt angry blisters on her forehead, cheeks, and chin.

Behind them, the forest was in flames.

"Grrrrrooool-th-th-th!" said Franklin as he sloshed and splattered, half-submerged.

"What's wrong?" Chantal said, stroking his nose.

Franklin shuddered softly as she ran her hand over the bumps and knobs and small domes like buttons. His skin, having lost its gloss and shine, had a weathered look. His breathing was labored. His leather harness was gone.

Chantal studied his eyes, and the eyes stared back weakly. She winked and Franklin winked back slowly. He was obviously in pain.

"Where are you hurt?" she said.

Chantal stood and gazed down Franklin's flank. Blood was in the water from a wound in his side, a wound the size and shape of a horseshoe.

"Oh, Franklin!"

She splashed through the water and touched the wound ever so gently. Franklin shuddered and let out a groan.

The wound looked deep and serious. From it surged

a spurt of bright scarlet. It must have been caused by a bomb. Metal fragments of the shell still remained.

"We have to get you some help."

The moment she said it, she realized it was a stupid thing to say. They were in the middle of the wilderness. In the middle of a war zone. There would be no veterinarians in such a situation. Not even a doctor.

Chantal was Franklin's only hope.

41

BLOWN TO BITS

Light broke through the branches in frail rays. Chantal sat staring at it until the sun rose above the treetops. She felt completely inadequate to be someone's only hope.

She glanced back down the Seine with thoughts of returning to Rouen. Maybe she could find help for Franklin there. Parts of the forest had been blown to bits, with fallen trees blocking sections of the river. Farther down was a smoky image of destruction. Was that the city?

A terrifying thought crushed Chantal: The bombs—had they flattened Rouen?

Had Colonel Myles been able to free Papa and Aunt Sophie in time?

Or had they been killed in the raid?

Chantal buried her face in her hands, wanting to cry, but her tears had been burned dry by the fireballs. Her throat clenched nonetheless.

Was she all alone?

Her mind raced with questions and uncertainties. If Papa or Aunt Sophie needed her help, she should return to Rouen. But even if she decided to turn around and could convince Franklin to do the same, their way back was an elaborate obstacle course at best.

She listened to the whale, his sighs and shivers. He was all she had left. If she didn't take care of him, he'd never survive. Whatever had happened in Rouen was beyond her control. But here she could still make a difference. Franklin needed her more than ever. What could she do?

Her rucksack floated to shore. After unstrapping the wet flaps, she found her mother's ukulele inside, smashed to pieces. Chantal picked them up sadly. The neck was snapped in two. Most of the ivory pegs were missing. The remaining strands of mother-of-pearl inlay sparkled with one last glint of promise.

How thoughtless she'd been to bring Mama's precious ukulele on such a dangerous voyage. The instrument that had bonded the three of them together.

Chantal squeezed the pieces in her hands, scraps of wood held together by lengths of metal string. She squeezed them until her fingers ached and the metal sliced into her skin.

Metal string!

Quickly she untangled the ukulele strings from the remaining bits of the instrument's body. With the thickest string, Chantal dug the bomb shards out of Franklin's skin. He shuddered each time she did this, but he was calm and courageous.

"Now comes the hardest part," she warned.

He let out a few squawks in anticipation.

Chantal took the thinnest, most delicate string and approached Franklin's wound.

"I have to stitch it up," she explained, "otherwise it might become infected."

Franklin let out two *dook*s and grumbled.

"It will hurt, but only for a short while. Afterward, you'll heal and get better. Understand?"

Franklin let out a high squeak and made several clicking sounds in a row. Chantal hoped this meant "Okay."

She touched him and felt the trust rush between them.

After Chantal had sewn up Franklin's wound, he lay still for hours. There was no way for her to know whether he was angry or he'd grasped the necessity of what she'd done.

Chantal waited for him to heal. In the meantime, she gathered the largest fish that had been killed by the bombs. Franklin refused to eat any of her catch, so she roasted the fish over a fire and made a meal for herself. Whenever the smoke drifted toward Franklin, she fanned it away. She ate as much as she could. Not knowing how long she would be stranded, she wrapped up the leftovers in some sturdy leaves.

The day passed while Franklin slept half-submerged in the river. Although the night was dark and scary, Chantal didn't climb on his back seeking protection. She feared she might hurt him.

When the morning came, Franklin opened one of his eyes. Then the other.

Chantal's heart thrummed. "Franklin? Are you all right?"

No sound.

Franklin seemed in no better shape. She looked down the stretch of river that flowed toward the English Channel. His home couldn't be that far. They'd already traveled so many miles.

"Franklin, you're almost home."

No sound.

She let him rest, but by late afternoon Chantal was

losing patience. How could Franklin give up when he was so close?

"Wake up, Franklin."

He groaned.

"You have to wake up!"

His huge tail rose slightly as if he were planning to slap the water. Soon it eased uselessly back under the surface. Where was his gumption?

Chantal remembered Mama's words and repeated them to Franklin: "Part of growing up is not giving up."

Franklin bellowed a bit and blew some bubbles from his mouth.

"What do you mean, I don't know where we're going?" Chantal started pacing. "I know exactly where we're going, and you have to trust me."

Franklin cawed and chirped and made a rooting-pig sound that meant, "Stop!"

Chantal folded her arms across her chest. "Finally, I have your attention." She scurried on top of him and reached for the leather harness that wasn't there. How could she ride him without it? Her hopes were dashed, but she refused to let Franklin know.

"You and I are going that way"—she pointed down river—"where the Seine meets the English Channel. That's where you're from, or maybe even farther away. I don't know. You never told me."

Franklin cooed and trilled, and Chantal took it to mean, "Yes, farther away, but not much."

"Then show me," she said.

Franklin stirred. He let a long breath out of his blow-holes. She could feel his fins come to life, his tail batting steadily at the water.

"That's it. You can do it!"

Chantal flattened herself and gave him a four-limbed hug. With any luck, it would stop her from slipping of his back.

42

HOME

Chantal and Franklin traveled for the rest of the afternoon and into the early evening. She slipped, slid, and glided across his back, yet somehow managed to stay on.

He wasn't making it easy for her. Hungry as he was, Franklin swam and ate, and ate and swam, gobbling up fish left and right. What a gifted eater he was. Chantal could feel the force return to his fin strokes and the pumping beat of his tail.

When the English Channel finally broke across the

horizon, her pulse quickened. The sight was a stark and unexpected beauty, a seamless blue from water to sky.

Happiness rushed through her veins.

Yet on the heels of this happiness, a chill trickled down her spine. Something heavy skidded across the floor of her stomach. Something she'd been holding back ever since she promised Franklin to reunite him with his family.

Returning him to the sea meant the two of them saying good-bye.

"There it is, Franklin—home."

The Channel waited ahead of them like a mirage, a line of fate shimmering.

"Groootollsenne," said the whale.

She felt his great cheeks lift and push against her thighs, and she imagined that he was smiling.

Would his happiness make saying good-bye any easier?

In the distance, Honfleur became visible, the fishing town where Mama and Aunt Sophie had grown up. The closer Chantal got, the more she felt reassured. The old town by the sea looked to be intact, unharmed by the bombs.

When they finally passed it on the left side of the river, Chantal could make out the medieval buildings with their cross beams glowing orange in the early evening.

She also saw the stone jetty where she had waited so many years ago for her mother to return from the sea.

All at once she was seven years old again, hearing the empty boat knock against the jetty. She could feel Mama's Breton cap in her hands, its wool frayed and scratching her fingers.

She called up her mother's face and her recent words. *It's those left behind who suffer the most.*

How right Mama was.

Chantal thought about steering Franklin into the harbor and having him drop her off on the jetty. But she couldn't do that unnoticed. People would stare and point. They would want to meet Franklin. Some might even want to hurt him, like the hungry gardeners in Paris had.

It was best to let him go before anyone suspected he was there.

Chantal bypassed the town and continued until they reached the estuary. To the left of the wide river mouth was a rocky shore.

With a deep sigh, she scrambled off his back and onto a large flat boulder. There she lay on her stomach, pressing her lips to Franklin's nose. Her adorable whale, so full of courage and conviction. He'd always been a friend to her.

The time had come for her to be a friend to him. To set him free.

She hugged him one last time and pointed in the direction of the open sea.

"There it is. That's where you need to go."

Franklin's head followed her extended arm. He let out three ribbons of sound, like sorrow unfurling.

"I know," Chantal said. "I'll miss you too."

The sun was already setting. If she wanted to get back into town before dark, she'd have to leave soon.

Chantal stroked Franklin's head. His skin glowed again with health and radiance. How beautiful he was. It made her heart clench.

She hadn't thought it possible to love a whale, but she did. She loved his quiet intelligence and shy gaze. She loved his noble and contained calm. She loved his ethereal singing and all the busy noises he made. She loved his simple way of communicating through sounds and feelings and hunches and inklings. Through the meaningful silences only friends can share. Most of all, she loved his spirit.

She kissed him once more. It was time to let go.

"I love you, Franklin."

With two clicks, a bleat, and a whistle, he said it back. She knew he did.

It was the moment for him to swim away, but he hesitated.

"Go, Franklin. Find your family. I'm sure they miss you."

He grumbled.

"Don't worry about me. Papa and Aunt Sophie are waiting."

How she hoped these words were true.

"Go, Franklin. You won't be safe until you're at sea. Please, listen. I promise not to forget about you if you promise not to forget about me."

Franklin's giant heart, certain and kind, beat out a message that seemed to say, "I promise." He followed this with the *caw* of a raven and the *moo* of a cow.

Chantal smiled through her tears.

Whales understood the importance of a promise.

43

HONFLEUR

Chantal moved away from the shore and climbed the hill behind the town. From there, she could better watch Franklin make his voyage out to sea, and also pay a visit to a special someone.

On top of the hill was the cemetery where they had buried Mama. Chantal, Papa, and Aunt Sophie had chosen this spot so Mama would always have a view of the sea.

Chantal reached the cemetery gates and looked back. There Franklin was, swimming strong, making his way toward a darker patch of blue farther out. He seemed to know where he was going and be in a hurry to get there.

Good for him.

With a heavy heart, Chantal threaded between the rows of graves until she came to her mother's and stopped. The wind lifted and chilled Chantal to the bone.

It began to dawn on her that her worst fears might be true. Her letter had never been delivered to Papa and Aunt Sophie. Colonel Myles had failed. The city of Rouen had been bombed and destroyed.

She was truly alone. If she descended into the town, she would find Aunt Sophie's house boarded up and abandoned.

No one was coming to meet her.

She shielded her eyes with her hand and looked out to where Franklin was swimming. At least he was finally home.

Chantal placed her hand on Mama's tombstone. For a second, she felt something within the stone rise forward to touch her: a hand, a blue light, floating straight into her eyes.

It was her mother's courage, her confidence when tackling a challenge. Chantal would need every bit of this courage in the days to come.

"Mama, if you had known that Papa and Aunt Sophie were never coming back, that I would be alone forever, would you have let me stay with you?"

Chantal waited for a response, but none came. "If I had known, would I have wanted to stay?"

The tombstone remained silent. She had never talked to Mama so seriously before, like a grown-up. As it turned out, Mama was a good listener.

Chantal thought about the questions her mother couldn't answer for her. She screwed up her face with resolve. "You were right to send me back to the surface. As much as I wanted to stay with you under the water, I need to live. I want to live. I'm certain you understand."

The tears she'd been holding back came in a torrent. She didn't know whether she was crying more for having survived or for being alone.

Through her tears, she watched the sun touch the horizon and glitter like a kaleidoscope across the water. The wind picked up. Where would she sleep tonight? Among the graves, in an empty tomb?

"We thought we'd find you here."

Chantal whipped around.

Papa was on crutches and Aunt Sophie had her arm in a sling. They were alive!

Chantal ran and embraced them both at the same time. Papa's smell of tobacco and leather mixed with the cork and clove of Aunt Sophie. Home. How tightly they held on to one another! Chantal didn't ever want to let them go.

Eventually she did, if only to look them in the eye and

make sure they were real and here. Aunt Sophie clucked her tongue as she smoothed back what was left of Chantal's singed hair. Papa joined in, petting Chantal's head in the way that used to annoy her. Now it didn't annoy her at all. Not one bit.

They exchanged smiles and tears. No questions, no reproof. It was enough to love and be loved, the most powerful force in the world.

Chantal turned to gaze out across the Channel. Franklin was still swimming. Not far from him, she began to see larger and darker shapes, much bigger than Franklin. Her heart skipped at least two beats.

The polished backs of whales burst through the surface.

"Look!" Chantal called out, pointing at the massive, heaving shapes. What a large family Franklin had!

Just like Chantal, he was surrounded by his loved ones.

"You did it, *ma chou*," said Aunt Sophie.

"Unbelievable," Papa whispered. "I'm so proud of you."

"Grrrrrooool-th-th-th!" came to them across the ocean. "Grrrrrooool-th-th-th!" the whales called in unison.

That sound was the first call Chantal had ever heard from Franklin. Perhaps this was their signature. Their family song. What they called out to one another when one of the pod was lost.

As loud as she could, Chantal threw her voice into the wind, calling back, "Grrrrrooool-th-th-th!"

Papa and Aunt Sophie joined Chantal. "Grrrrrooool-th-th-th! Grrrrrooool-th-th-th!"

And then they laughed.

Franklin's family, with him swimming in its center, moved farther and farther away until their fins stroking the air could hardly be distinguished from the whitecaps. The sunset was glowing with impossible, shifting colors.

Chantal waved good-bye one last time.

Papa and Aunt Sophie waved at Franklin too.

Home was a feeling, not a place. It was where your family was, where you were known and loved.

Chantal took the photograph from her pocket, the one that showed all four of them together, and placed it on the grave like a bouquet of flowers. Miraculously, the photograph seemed untouched by all the violence she'd experienced.

Aunt Sophie regarded Chantal curiously. She stooped down to get a closer look at the picture. Tears trailed down her face. Papa placed his arm around Sophie.

In that instant, Chantal realized that the four of them were in the same configuration as they had been in the photo: Sophie's hand touching Mama's tombstone, with Papa's arm slung around her, and Chantal in the middle.

Where she belonged.

EPILOGUE

Chantal and Papa stayed with Aunt Sophie in Honfleur. The war in Normandy was over, which wasn't the case for the rest of France.

On August twenty-fifth, the Americans finally arrived in Paris. Chantal cheered and cried when she heard the news. The troops marched through a city that had already been freed by the Resistance.

But there would be another year of war before the rest of Europe was free.

During that time, Chantal and Papa returned home, where Odette's mother and the gardeners apologized for their behavior. Chantal forgave them. She might have pardoned Father Maurice, too, if he hadn't been sent to another parish somewhere far away.

Who had time for grudges? There was much to do now that the war was over.

"Fresh fish!"

The rattle of cart wheels on cobblestones. Ice tingling her fingertips. The clack of the scales. Wherever Chantal and Papa went with their cart of fresh fish, people came in a hurry. The Duprey family had the freshest fish in all of Paris.

And why shouldn't they? Aunt Sophie brought it by the bucketful three times a week from Normandy.

Life was almost back to the way it was before the war, except that Mama wasn't there to play her ukulele and sing. Now it was Chantal's job to entertain the customers. Papa had bought her a new ukulele to replace the one that had been destroyed.

People laughed and danced while waiting for their fish. Chantal felt glad and hopeful, even though part of her heart was with Franklin and the open sea.

The anniversary of D-day approached, and the town of Honfleur was planning a celebration. Aunt Sophie knew the demand for fresh fish would be high, so she asked Chantal and Papa to come and help her with the catch. The three of them went out in the boat on June third to get started, but they caught almost nothing—a big disappointment. When the same thing occurred the following day, Aunt Sophie grew worried. What would they have to sell?

Chantal came up with a wonderful but secret plan. On June fifth, she asked Sophie to steer the boat to where they'd seen Franklin rejoin his family last summer. The sun shone bright between tatters of clouds. When they reached the spot in the English Channel, Chantal said, "Stop the motor, please."

Papa arched an eyebrow, but Sophie did as Chantal asked. The *Victoire* rocked to the sound of the wind and the gulls. Chantal climbed onto the bow, cupped her hands around her mouth, and called, "Grrrrrooool-th-th-th!"

And again: "Grrrrrooool-th-th-th!"

Nothing returned the call.

But Chantal was no quitter. From her rucksack, she removed her ukulele and strummed the first two chords of "Somewhere Over the Rainbow."

The water around the boat sloshed. Her heart danced with energy. An antsy sensation trickled down her spine. Before long, a dark shape broke through the surface with a splash.

"Grrrrrooool-th-th-th!"

Franklin! He nudged up to the side of the boat so that Chantal could embrace him.

"Oh, I've missed you!" she said, wrapping her arms around as much of him as she could reach. Her happiness was as wide as the sea and just as wild.

"Yeeeeoooooowwwwwl," said Franklin, flapping up an excited spray with his fins. Had he grown since last year? Chantal thought so.

Papa and Sophie leaned over the side of the *Victoire* to give him a pat.

While they were distracted, Chantal climbed onto Franklin's back. She was wearing her rubber boots and life vest, after all.

"Cherie!" Papa shouted, worried.

"It's okay," Chantal said. "Start the engine and follow us!"

"Get back in the boat, right now!"

"Everything will be fine," she said. "C'mon, Franklin. Let's go fishing!"

With Chantal hugging his back, Franklin took off, swimming faster than she'd expected. Her pulse quickened. Blood rushed to her cheeks. It took a moment for her to adjust, but when she did, riding him was just like old times. The best place to be was on the back of her friend.

The boat stayed right on his tail. After a short while, Chantal could feel his jaw slant downward.

She waved her hand and shouted back to the *Victoire*. "Drop the nets!"

So that's what Papa and Sophie did.

Chantal filled her lungs until she was dizzy with joy. The four of them were the perfect fisherteam. Bliss like a golden chord threaded through her body. Wind lifted her hair and bathed her face in ocean spray. Franklin's fins churned the water. And love stirred Chantal's heart, love for her family, above and under the sea.

ACKNOWLEDGMENTS

For her time and expertise and enormous enthusiasm, we are forever grateful to Marie Lamba, our agent—your kindness is an inspiration. Special thanks also to Jennifer de Chiara for warmly welcoming us to the agency.

For her passion and dedication, for championing our novel from the start, our profound thanks go to Reka Simonsen, our editor at Atheneum. Thanks also go to Julia McCarthy, the super-sharp copy editors Clare McGlade and Jeannie Ng, and the rest of the Atheneum team for making this book happen, and to Erin McGuire, who brought it to life with her gorgeous illustrations.

For their endless support and affection, we'd like to thank our families and friends—it's a gift to know you are there, believing in us. Special thanks go to those who have opened their homes to us as private writing retreats: the Tillmann family (Martin and Eva, Regina and David, from Jolimont to Los Angeles), Karolina Blåberg, Régis Roinsard and Valerie Taylor, Monique and Rob van Damien, Lori Mozilo and Ken Karman, and anyone else we have regretfully overlooked.

Last but not least, an immense thanks to our readers—this book is for you.